to Alicia:
Happy Skating!

by **Cherie** **Wein**

Cherie Wein

Dedication

This book is dedicated to award-winning science fiction author
Joe Pumilia, who years ago helped me when I did not deserve it.
The man has the patience of a saint.

that ran next to the street called Cedar Terrace, which was also the name of the development where her mother lived. Cindy skated toward the entrance to the development, feeling good for a bunch of reasons.

It was summertime, so no school. It was Saturday and she had spent the day with her mom. She was staying with her mom in Murrayville, Maryland, where she felt safer than back in Baltimore with her father and his family. And she didn't have to put up with her stepmother or that noisy brat of a baby.

Cindy bent her knees way down, then jumped up high in the air. She stuck her legs straight out to the sides and reached her fingertips to touch her toes in what ice skaters called a "Russian split." Then she tucked her legs beneath her body, twisted halfway around, and landed backwards on both feet. Cindy knew she was a good skater.

She rolled backwards past a half-dozen nearly identical townhouses. They all had tiny front lawns and lots of cedar trees in the open spaces between them. The townhouses were more than twenty years old, which was why her mom could afford to buy one. Even with her new software certification, Cindy's mother didn't make a lot of money.

Cindy turned forward again and set up a rhythm to T-Bird's song. In a strip where there were no cars, she jumped down to the asphalt and back up to the sidewalk for four parking spaces, keeping the fast beat the whole time. *Look what I can do!* she thought, wishing her friend Amanda were there to watch.

Things were so much better now than they were after the divorce three years ago. Back then her parents sold the house and her mom went back to school for computer certification. Cindy had to live at her dad's high-rise apartment in downtown Baltimore. When she was at his place, she skated in the streets and nearby parks where tough kids hung out and picked on her—the same kind of tough kids she had to put up with in school every day. Back then her mom could only afford a tiny studio apartment in a cheap part of town. Cindy visited her every other weekend, but she had to put up with more rough kids there.

But I sure can take care of myself! Nobody messes with me anymore and it's nice that here in Murrayville nobody's even tried. Maybe Mom'll get a raise and dad can pay more child support money so I can stay here all year.

Cindy wished she could be like T-Bird, who was only fifteen years old and already a multimillionaire.

Cindy reached the traffic light where Cedar Terrace met busy Turnberry Avenue. Across Turnberry was the Murrayville Library, closed this late on a weekend day. Cindy went there a lot to find books and use the computers. To the left of the library's large parking lot the land sloped slightly upward to the grounds of Grace Evangelical Church, a big orange brick building hidden by tall trees. That was where her friend Amanda Carter's family went to church each Sunday; Cindy had gone along a couple of times.

Right now Cindy was not planning to cross Turnberry. She went right, the opposite direction from the church, crossed Cedar Terrace, and jumped the curb to the sidewalk. She was going to skate toward Smallwood Lane, where there was a development called Evergreen Woods with lots of long sidewalks. Her mom wouldn't want her going there because there wasn't a traffic light. Mom always insisted Cindy cross streets at the traffic lights.

"Last year a woman was killed when she crossed down there where there wasn't a light." Mom had lectured her the way she always did, with her short arms bent, hands on her hips, and her roundish face stern the way it was when she meant it. She wasn't much taller than Cindy these days.

"Come on, Mom!" Cindy had answered. "I heard that story already from Amanda. It happened just down the street at Turnberry and Smallwood. But the traffic is just as bad in Baltimore and I haven't gotten hurt."

"Baltimore has lots of short blocks and lights for cars to stop at," Mom had insisted. "Murrayville has long roads with curves that you can't see around. There's a blind curve down there where she was killed. Cars come hurtling around there and don't have time to stop. So I want you to wait at a light."

But her mom had it wrong because the car that killed that lady had been going the same way Cindy was, not coming from the other direction.

"Cindy!" shouted a voice. Cindy looked around to see a familiar blue van turning into the development. A slim, coffee-colored hand waved from the back seat and an African-American girl smiled. "I like your new hairdo!"

It was Amanda Carter, Cindy's new best friend. Amanda's cornrows and long beaded braids looked neat despite her having swum in them. Amanda's mother and her little brother Tayvon chorused "Hi!" from the other side of the van, while her smiling father called, "Hello there, Miss Cindy!" The Carters had moved into the neighborhood in May, not long before Cindy arrived in June.

"Hey, Amanda!" Cindy called back. That was something else she liked: it was easy to make friends here.

The Carters' van drove along toward their townhouse, a block past Cindy's and on the other side of the street. Cindy could have gone swimming and out to dinner with Amanda and her family, but instead she'd gone to the hair stylist's with Mom. Afterward they had gone to a pizza place for supper and then the store to buy groceries for the week. Once they got home it was Cindy's chance to do something on her own—go street skating.

Cindy pushed west into the sun, toward Smallwood Lane.

•••

I wish I felt like going out to skate with her.

Amanda watched Cindy skating away until the view of Turnberry was cut off. Soon they were at her own townhouse, across the street and down from Cindy's, and her father was pulling into their assigned parking space. Other cars were arriving home from their Saturday outings. Kids were coming out to ride their bicycles, and parents were bringing toddlers to the playground that sat in the open space at the end of the Carters' block. Amanda's brother Tayvon was anxious to get out and join them; he bounced up and down in his seat belt, his left bare foot kicking Amanda and his waving arm banging into her head.

"Stop it!" she shouted.

"Tayvon, behave!" snapped Amanda's mother.

Amanda and her family had come from Chicago, where she'd grown up in a huge neighborhood containing street after street of nothing but African-American families. Here in Murrayville, at least in Cedar Terrace, were Asians, Caucasians, Hindus, African-Americans, and all kinds of nationalities. Amanda felt blessed to live in a place where so many different kinds of families lived next door to each other, where the kids got along so well, playing together constantly. It was something new for Amanda. She and Cindy had made friends right away, almost the first day Cindy had come to the neighborhood.

Amanda hoped she never moved away from Murrayville. It had to be the most perfect place in the world to live.

She grabbed the bundle that held her pink towel and pink swimsuit, and followed her family up to the house. She really wanted to come back outside and try to catch Cindy. But she was tired. She felt she just had to relax for the rest of the evening.

If her little brother Tayvon would leave her alone.

• • •

A slightly slower song began in Cindy's ears, "U R 2 Much," but it was still a fast beat. T-Bird's soft voice, with its occasional squeak, sang the modulated words in Cindy's ears:

> Don't think that you're a loser,
> Don't ever give up.
> Just keep on tryin' harder,
> 'Cause U R 2 Much!

It was when T-Bird performed the video to this song that she wore in-line skates, a blue tank top, tight jeans, and bandannas on her arms.

Just like I'm dressed right now, except I'm wearing shorts because it's too hot for jeans.

Faster, faster, faster! Cindy jumped in the air again, twisted around in a 360 turn, and landed forward on both feet, keeping total time to the music. Before her the sidewalk sloped gently downward so her speed increased without any effort. Cedar trees sped past, hiding the other Cedar Terrace townhouses and shielding them from street noise.

She turned backward and did some fancy foot moves, crossing each foot in front of the other in time to the beat. She stepped forward, jumped up in the air, and landed backward on her right foot with her left knee bent in a stylized pose and her arms out to the sides. She held the position for a long, long moment, waving her arms and watching the evergreens next to the sidewalk whiz away on her left.

The song was short, only about two minutes. When it was over, Cindy was really winded and sweat was streaming down her forehead and cheeks.

I wish I'd brought my sunglasses, because that sun is shining right in my face.

A really slow song started, "Cool Wind." T-Bird wailed, but not the way Cindy's baby stepbrother Peter did. Cindy turned backward and performed grace-ful, elongated moves with her feet and arms in time to the music. She raised arms toward the sky, which was a beautiful blue and had white fluffy clouds that looked so low she could have touched them.

Along the other side of Turnberry Avenue were tall deciduous trees, the spaces between them filled with undergrowth and vines. Beyond the trees were thick woods, and somewhere past the woods, she knew, was Smallwood Mansion, a historic landmark where a rich family lived. The upcoming street, where the lady had been killed the year before, and the neighborhood around the mansion, were all famous for being named for the Smallwoods.

Cindy twisted both feet to turn forward. She had reached Smallwood Lane. The sun was really in her eyes now. As she dug in her heel brakes and stopped at the intersection, a white Cadillac turned out from the other side of Turnberry. Cindy shaded her eyes. The car was driven by a gray-haired man wearing a black uniform hat. A blond-haired girl sat in the back seat. Cindy could make out an adult sitting on the far side of the back seat, a woman, she thought.

Cindy had seen the car and the girl several times before, but always in the mornings. Now the girl looked directly at Cindy, then away, without even an acknowledgment. She always did that.

Once Amanda had been with Cindy. She had pointed at the car window. "That's Jennifer Smallwood, that stuck-up rich girl who lives in Smallwood Mansion. She goes to The Ice House in Fern Oak every morning. My Dad says professional ice skaters give expensive lessons there. She's won some ice skating competitions."

"Where does she go to school?" The girl looked about the same age as Cindy and Amanda.

"At Fitzhugh Academy, a girls' school." Amanda had shaken her head and the beads on her braids had clicked together. "Dad says it's a really expensive place."

"I wonder if the other girls there are friendly," Cindy had commented, "because she's certainly not."

Now Cindy stared after the car with the solemn, blond-haired girl in it and wondered what it was like to be rich.

●●●

That girl looks just like T-Bird! thought Jennifer Smallwood. She wondered what the girl's name was and where she lived. Ever since school had let out

Jennifer had noticed the brown-haired girl skating almost every day, sometimes with a friend, sometimes alone. Today the girl's hair was short and spiked, and she was dressed almost the way T-Bird did in her video "U R 2 Much."

How nice it must be, Jennifer thought, to go anywhere you wanted, not to have to be driven everywhere by your chauffeur. And just hang out with friends—what freedom!

But she didn't have very many friends. What was the point? She could never spend time with them anyway. Her mother had set a course for her, and she was not allowed to do anything that deviated from that course, including having fun.

Right now she and her mother were going out to a restaurant. After that they might go to a movie, but probably not. Lately Mrs. Smallwood no longer liked to sit in theaters. Jennifer thought her mother just didn't like being around ordinary people, and Lorraine Smallwood always emphasized that their family was not ordinary.

Jennifer looked away from the skating girl and started to sigh. Then she stopped herself. Her mother would ask her why, and Jennifer did not feel like answering any questions.

* * *

Cindy watched the big Cadillac drive away, growing smaller until it passed the street light at the library and Cedar Terrace. It joined other cars that were climbing the slope of Turnberry Avenue past Grace Evangelical Church. Finally the Cadillac disappeared to the left around one of those curves Mom had warned about.

Cindy looked at the sky. *Almost time to go home! I need to skate a little more first.* Cindy pushed off quickly into Evergreen Woods, but then slowed when she saw somebody watching her.

A lady stood on a patch of grass next to the sidewalk, smiling. The lady looked older than Cindy's mother, maybe ten years. Her light-colored hair was styled in a puff around her face. She wore a pale blue dress and high-heeled shoes the same color. Most striking of all were her pale green eyes, which seemed to glow even in the glare of the lowering sun.

The lady was saying something; the loud music interfered, so Cindy pulled off her headset to hear.

"You're pretty good," the lady said.

"Thank you." Cindy didn't always talk to strangers, but this lady seemed extremely nice and totally harmless.

"How long have you been skating?"

"About a year, since my dad gave me these skates."

"Do you ever skate inside a rink?"

Cindy shook her head. "Rinks are no fun. They're too crowded with people and they don't have enough room."

Cindy pressed her right foot forward and her left foot back until she began turning in a slow circle. Then she tightened her feet closer and pulled her arms into her waist so that she spun faster. After several revolutions she stiffened her legs, stuck her arms out, and came to a quick stop, still in the same spot on the sidewalk.

"Did somebody teach you that?"

"No, I learned it on my own by watching ice skaters on TV."

The lady nodded, as if she had expected the answer.

"Cindy, would you please do something for me?"

Startled, Cindy almost said, "How do you know my name?" But she looked into the woman's green eyes and couldn't do anything but nod.

"Would you go to the Roller Haven Roller Rink on Broadway and see a lady named Barbara McAllister? She owns the rink and she used to be a champion competitive roller skater. I think you should talk to her."

Cindy was about to say no, or just agree so the lady would leave her alone. But instead she found herself nodding and meaning it. "All right."

The lady's smile grew bigger. "Oh, that's wonderful. Be sure to tell Barbara that Mary Jo sent you, okay?"

Cindy nodded. "Um, okay, I guess."

"I have to go now. Thanks for talking to me."

"You're welcome. 'Bye." Cindy rolled a few feet forward along the sidewalk, then twirled around backward, facing Mary Jo.

But she was gone. The patch of grass next to the sidewalk was empty. And there was no house the lady could have run to or car she could have gotten into nearby.

"Weird!" Cindy said, staring.

Suddenly she wanted very much to go to that roller skating rink.

Chapter 2
The Roller Haven

"I'll be here to pick you both up at 4:00 when session is over. Don't wander off anywhere." Cindy's Mom sat at the wheel of her old green Toyota. Her face was red and her dark hair damp from driving in the heat, but the brown eyes behind her tortoise-shell plastic-rimmed glasses were wide-open in warning.

"Oh, Mom, where would we go?" Cindy waved a bandanna-tied arm. "There aren't any malls or movies or anything here, there's just that old thrift store across the road and a used car shop next door, so there's not anything else to do but stay here at the rink."

The used car lot was on the other side of a chain link fence and was very strange looking. Its yellow stucco building had two colorful, mosaic-tiled towers and some big, added-on rooms made of bare wooden planks. The thrift shop across the street sat between an empty, overgrown field and a run-down motel.

Valerie Buford nodded. "Right. So don't go off looking for anything else, you hear?"

Cindy was about to make a smart answer, but Amanda poked her in the back. "We won't, Mrs. Buford. See you at four."

"Goodbye, girls." Cindy's mother circled the asphalt parking lot to its entrance, then turned onto Broadway and drove away. Cindy and Amanda hung the tied laces of their in-line skates across their shoulders and got into a line before the orange-painted, concrete block rink. The line was full of children waiting to skate the Sunday afternoon session. A lot of them carried wrapped presents and held their parents' hands.

"Looks like somebody's birthday party," commented Amanda. Her pink tank shirt was just like Cindy's blue one.

"I just hope I don't trip over all these little kids while I'm skating," grumbled Cindy.

They reached the ticket window to pay admission. A lady with gray hair tied back in a long braid checked their skates before they could take them inside. "Sometimes the brakes can put black marks or even scratches in the floor," she explained. "Both of yours are okay."

"Is Barbara McAllister here?" asked Cindy.

"She's inside. Do you need to see her about a party?"

"I just want to ask her about skating."

The woman pressed a buzzer so the door beside the ticket window unlocked. Amanda pushed open the door and they entered the rink.

The walls inside were painted blue and gray. There was a blue carpet on the floor in front of them. They moved over to a waist-high, gray concrete barrier that surrounded the skating floor. The skating floor was of smooth light-colored wood and coated with shiny lacquer. There were several entrances through the barrier to get onto the floor.

Farther down to the girls' right, adults and little kids crowded the space in front of a window with a sign that read "Skate Room." They were getting rental skates. Past the skate room was a sign that said "Restrooms," and two doors in the concrete block walls.

The two girls walked across the blue carpeting to a long wooden bench where they sat and put their skates on. "I've been in places like this," said Amanda, "when I was really young. But they didn't look this nice."

They left their shoes in cubbyholes underneath the bench, then stood and tried to roll across the carpet. Cindy was surprised. "This stuff really slows you down."

"Probably to keep people from falling," said Amanda.

Hardly anybody was skating yet. Cindy and Amanda passed through an opening in the concrete wall and began chasing each other around the skating floor to the loud rap music.

A man's voice came over the loudspeaker. "No racing, please. Don't go any faster than you can easily stop." They saw an elderly man with a big gray mustache watching them from an announcer's booth near the front door. A sign over the door into the booth read "Office." Next to the booth was a snack bar, and in front of the snack bar were three decorated party tables, each filled with presents and a birthday cake.

Cindy grimaced at his words. "I can stop no matter how fast I go."

"Don't be mean. They might kick us out."

"I don't know if I like it here because this going 'round and 'round in the same circle is boring. Skating outdoors is better."

"We don't have to come back after today," Amanda pointed out.

The music changed to another popular song with a fast beat. More skaters came onto the floor, mostly parents holding little kids' hands, though many of the parents could hardly stand up. Soon the floor was filled with people from those birthday parties, all wearing ugly brown rental skates and constantly getting in the two girls' way.

"I'm already tired of dodging little kids," complained Cindy.

"Let's go get something to drink."

They left the floor and rolled to the snack bar. A woman was handing out nachos, slices of pizza, candy bars, and soda, and taking money from a long line of customers. Cindy and Amanda waited their turns, then ordered sodas. While they were paying, Cindy asked, "Is Barbara here?"

"I'm Barbara." The short, slender woman had dark red hair in a pixie style. Her brown eyes were friendly; she smiled and gave them their change, then held two ice-filled plastic cups under separate soda spigots.

"Hi, I'm Cindy Buford. This is Amanda Carter."

"Nice to meet you." The sodas were full. Barbara pulled them away from the spigots.

"A lady named Mary Jo sent me," continued Cindy.

Barbara jerked and glanced at them quickly, her eyes wide. Soda sloshed over the top of each cup and onto the counter. She stood there with soda rolling down each hand.

"Did you say 'Mary Jo'?" She almost whispered.

"Yes, that's right." Cindy glanced at Amanda, wondering if she should have kept quiet.

Barbara seemed to remember the drinks. She set them on the counter, then reached for a damp cloth and began to wipe the outsides of the cups. Her face had become pale.

"Is something wrong?" asked Cindy, taking her drink. Cindy looked over at Amanda, who was staring at Barbara in amazement.

Barbara stared at the counter as she wiped it. "Are . . . you sure you're not mistaken?"

"No, that's what she said."

Then Barbara frowned slightly and looked at both girls with suspicion. "Well, take your drinks and go." She turned away and started toward the other end of the counter.

"Wait!" said Cindy. "Who was Mary Jo?"

Barbara at first didn't answer, just looked mad. Then she said, "As if you didn't know, she used to be a skater here." She pointed toward the end wall beyond the party tables. The girls saw many large, framed posters of skaters. "There's her picture."

"She doesn't skate any more?" asked Cindy.

"Give me a break." Now Barbara looked as if she were about to cry. She disappeared into the office.

"Wow, that was weird," said Amanda.

"Yeah, and rude too. Come on, let's look at the pictures."

They threaded among tables, parents, and children to stare up at the wall. There were posters of about a dozen people wearing skates and extravagantly-decorated skating costumes. Banners over their heads said things like "USA National Championships," and Barbara McAllister stood in the picture with almost every skater. They found one poster showing a woman who matched the description Cindy had given Amanda of Mary Jo.

"Is this the lady?" asked Amanda, pointing to one.

"I think so," answered Cindy.

"She sure is wearing a pretty costume."

Mary Jo's costume was sparkly pink and had long tight sleeves; green jewels shone on the bodice and sleeves. Her reddish-blond hair was in the same puffy style as when Cindy had spoken to her. Cindy couldn't make out her eye color. Beside her in the picture, Barbara McAllister had on a black pantsuit and high heels.

"The banner over her head says that was two years ago," commented Amanda. "I wonder if she still skates."

"Barbara said she doesn't," Cindy answered absently. She was studying the other posters. In one, a boy in a shirt with puffy red sleeves and tight black pants posed with a girl in a short red skating dress. There were pictures of men and women, boys and girls, standing alone or in couples. They wore costumes in every imaginable color, all of them heavily decorated with sequins and jewels.

"Barbara is in every one of them," commented Amanda.

"I wonder what you have to do to like get your picture up there?" wondered Cindy.

"It looks like you have to buy a fancy costume."

Against the wall were some booths for people who weren't attending any of the parties. The girls sat in one and drank their sodas, and then went back onto the floor.

During the session they joined in with the Limbo and the Electric Slide. They skated together twice during "Couples Only," when the lights were dimmed and a big mirrored globe lit up the floor. There was even a "shoot-the-duck" contest, where people squatted down on one skate and held the other leg straight ahead until only one person was left still rolling. The little kids weren't very good at it; in the end only Cindy and Amanda were left rolling, and finally Amanda fell over sideways. Cindy won a certificate for a free slice of pizza. She and Amanda shared the slice.

When the session was nearly over, the little kids and parents left the floor to take off their skates.

Cindy said, "Look, the floor's empty. Now we can have some room to skate!" The two girls went back out to skate; only a floor guard in a black and white striped shirt was out there with them.

Just then, T-Bird's song "U R 2 Much" came over the loudspeaker. Cindy gasped and smiled. She pushed faster and began doing the kinds of moves she used on the sidewalks. To the first verse, she turned 'round and 'round on one foot while going down the floor, then did the Russian splits. When the second verse started, she skated backwards and crossed her feet back and forth, waving and circling her arms with the music.

You know you are a winner,
You've got the magic touch.
You're going to the top now,
Because U R 2 much!

She jumped up, turned one and a half times, and landed forward on one foot. As the music played, Cindy's energy grew. She kept going faster and faster around the floor, doing more and more intricate turns and jumps. Through it all she imitated the choreography and moves T-Bird had used in her video.

The song drew to a close. Cindy slowed and did that two-foot spin she had learned from watching ice skating on TV. She stopped right as the music ended, and a huge burst of applause broke out.

Cindy left the floor smiling. "You're real good!" said the watching little kids.

Barbara McAllister skated up to her. "That was great! Where did you learn that?"

"I just kind of taught myself."

"You're almost ready for Creative Solo competition."

"What's that?"

"It's a skating contest. You compete against other people skating to music. But you would need to change and add a few things to your routine."

"Routine?"

"Your program. Ice skaters say 'program,' roller skaters say 'routine.'"

"Wow. You think I'm good enough?"

"You could be. Why don't you talk to your parents about it and see what they say?"

"What about my skating?" asked Amanda. "Do you think I could compete?"

Barbara cocked her head to one side. "I think you could be a good racer. You're very fast."

Amanda shoved a fist into the air. "Yeah!"

They were taking off their skates when the announcer with the big gray mustache walked by.

"Excuse me, sir?" asked Cindy. "We were looking at those pictures on the wall. That lady in pink–who is she?"

"Oh, that's–or *was*–Mary Jo Green. She was a national solo dance champion. Took lessons from my daughter Barbara for years. Good skater."

Amanda asked, "Why did you say it *was* Mary Jo Green?"

"Well, she died in a car accident just about a year ago."

Chapter 3
Bedtime

That night, Jennifer Smallwood sat in an antique green brocade chair and surfed the net with the computer that sat on her mahogany escritoire. Green velvet curtains covered the window. Behind her was an antique four-poster bed. The whole house was furnished with antiques. The only modern-looking touches in Jennifer's room were the computer and the portable television that sat on one end of her dressing table.

Her eyes were drooping, but she kept searching for pictures of her favorite singer/rap star, T-Bird. A knock sounded at her bedroom door. She minimized the window so that only some wallpaper of ice skaters was visible, then stood and went to the other end of the dressing table.

"Come in," she called.

The heavy bedroom door opened and an elderly woman in a black dress and white apron appeared. "Good evening, Jennifer."

"Hello, Mrs. Smith."

Mrs. Smith carried a glazed, flowered pitcher. She walked to the dresser and poured water from the pitcher into a matching bowl that sat there on a tray. Mrs. Smith and the chauffeur, Victor Smith, were married. They had worked for the Smallwood family since Jennifer's father was a boy.

Jennifer wet her hands in the water. It was lukewarm. She picked up a piece of handmade lavender-scented soap from a flowered ceramic soap dish on her dresser and began lathering. She rinsed her hands in the bowl of water and dried with an embroidered linen towel that lay on the tray.

She took her toothbrush from a flowered cup that matched the pitcher and bowl. She reached into a shallow drawer for a modern tube of toothpaste and squeezed some onto her brush, then scrubbed her teeth and spit into the bowl. Mrs. Smith poured clean water into a clear glass. Jennifer rinsed her mouth and spat again.

She wiped her mouth and placed the folded towel on the tray. Then she stood aside while Mrs. Smith took away the tray. As Mrs. Smith went through the open door, the lady asked, "Shall I tell your mother that you're ready for bed?"

"Yes, please."

Jennifer shut down the computer. Then she stood in front of the ornate mirror over her dresser and began brushing her long, golden hair with a golden hairbrush. Light came from a flowered glass lamp that sat across the room on the nightstand beside her bed. It lit up her bare arms and gleamed on the white silk nightgown with the pink rosebuds embroidered around the neckline.

The door opened and Jennifer's mother came in. "Hello, Dear." Jennifer placed her brush on the dresser and turned so Mrs. Smallwood could hug her. Lorraine Smallwood was tall, with long blonde hair like her daughter's. Roger Smallwood, Jennifer's father, was slightly taller, also blonde, and a little chubby. He was seldom at home.

Mrs. Smallwood stroked Jennifer's hair and gazed solemnly into her daughter's face. "How was skating practice today?"

"It was fine." Jennifer walked to her bed. The porcelain clock on the table beside the lamp read nine o'clock. She lay down and her mother pulled the heavy covers up and sat beside her. Then Jennifer rolled over and faced the wall.

"Jacques says you could win the Invitational next month." Jennifer had been practicing hard for that competition.

"Yes, if I don't fall down on the ice and break a bone, or jump in a river the day before."

"What a strange thing to say!" Mrs. Smallwood put a hand on her daughter's forehead. "Do you feel all right?" When Jennifer didn't answer, she continued,

"You're so lucky to take lessons from champion ice skaters. When I was a girl, I dreamt of wearing beautiful costumes and becoming a skating star." Mrs. Smallwood looked around the bedroom. "And I wanted a room of my own, full of beautiful things just like our ancestors in Colonial times."

Jennifer had heard all the stories about how poor her mother had been. "This house is more like what the rich French or British would have lived in. American colonists were like you. They didn't have any money."

Her mother's face froze. "Well, some of them did. And I'll thank you not to insult me like that."

"No one had electricity or air conditioning either. They would have been burning up on a humid night like this, not freezing like I am." Jennifer pulled the covers tighter. Her mother kept the house extremely cold in the summer.

Mrs. Smallwood frowned. "Jennifer, you are being very disagreeable!"

The girl didn't answer.

"Well, on that note, I will take my leave." Mrs. Smallwood rose and walked to the door. Then she paused with her hand on the old brass doorknob. "I hope you will go right to sleep. You have to get up early in the morning for your ballet lesson."

"As if I didn't know that already," Jennifer muttered.

"What?" Her mother's voice was sharp.

"Nothing. Good night, Mother."

"Good night." Her mother left and softly closed the door.

Jennifer turned off her lamp and sighed into the darkness. Why couldn't she find the courage to say to her mother, I *do not want to be an ice skating star.*

•••

Also that night, Amanda slept over at Cindy's house.

Amanda lay on Cindy's twin-sized bed in her pink sleep shirt. She was reading a dog-eared magazine with a picture of T-Bird on the cover. T-Bird's mouth was painted with bright red lipstick. She was smiling, with her arms and legs stuck out so she formed an "X." Her hair was short and black and stiff. She wore jeans and a bright aqua tank shirt and red bandannas tied around each arm. On her feet were in-line roller skates.

"It says here that T-Bird likes to sidewalk skate. Her skates cost a thousand dollars."

"Yeah, I saw that. My dad didn't pay anywhere near that much for my skates."

Cindy was dancing to a T-Bird song. She wore a yellow tee shirt that had been her father's and some old blue basketball shorts from her Baltimore gym class.

The only furniture in Cindy's room was a narrow bed and a matching white chest of drawers, both scratched and dull against the bare white walls. Cindy's mother could only afford used furniture for Cindy's room. There were no curtains on the window, just venetian blinds.

Amanda said, "That was really weird today."

"It freaked me out!" Cindy puffed. "That looked just like the same woman and I know she couldn't really be dead." She stopped and took a deep breath. Then she began doing jumping jacks. Her bare feet struck the beige shag carpet so that the floor shook.

"Don't you ever get tired?"

"Nope, never."

Cindy's mom came to the door. She wore a blue nightgown that she'd had when Cindy was only five years old. "Pipe down in here. It's bedtime!"

"Mom, this is summer and we don't have to go to school tomorrow."

"I still have to get up for work in the morning. I don't care how late you stay up, just keep quiet." She walked forward with her arms out and kissed and hugged Cindy. Then she said, "Remember, no noise." She went across the hall and closed her bedroom door behind her.

"Want to go downstairs and watch TV so Mom won't hear us?"

"Sounds good."

On the basement's worn brown carpeting, a lopsided couch and a battered beanbag cushion sat in front of an old television. There was nothing on TV so the girls switched to video games on Cindy's old Sega. When Amanda's eyes started drooping about one a.m., she said her bedtime prayers, then fell asleep on the couch. Cindy kept playing, suddenly missing her dad. She hadn't seen him, her stepmother Linda, or Peter, the baby, in a month. She hadn't even talked to them on the phone.

Her father usually didn't pay much attention to her. He'd given her the in-line skates last Christmas. Then at her birthday in April he'd given her some games for the Sega. They'd made a lot of noise playing the racecar game, laughing while they tried to beat each other.

But then Linda told them to keep quiet so they wouldn't wake the baby. Cindy had resented baby Peter because of things like that. He had made more noise when he was awake than Cindy ever did.

She was dozing off. The old-fashioned electrical clock sitting on the TV said it was almost three a.m. She shut off the Sega and flopped across the beanbag, where she promptly passed out.

And dreamed about a woman with puffy light hair and glowing green eyes, who had died a year ago but still talked to people.

Chapter 4
The Neighborhood

Jennifer got up Monday morning at six a.m. and was on her way to ballet class by seven, driven by Victor, the chauffeur. The air was a little foggy; it must have rained during the night because the streets were damp.

After two hours of dance class, Victor drove her to the ice rink, where she ate a brunch prepared early that morning by Victor's wife, Mrs. Smith. Jennifer took a free style lesson and had an hour of practice time. At one o'clock she arrived back at the circular driveway in front of her house, where Victor opened the car and house doors for her. He then drove the Cadillac past the house to a grove of maples, where he parked the car in the old barn, now converted into a five-car garage.

Jennifer, meanwhile, passed through the dark, heavily decorated house and entered the kitchen, looking for a snack.

Mrs. Smallwood, dressed in a white silk blouse and pale blue slacks, was sitting on a kitchen stool, giving the cook instructions. Mrs. Smallwood had probably sat there all morning; Jennifer couldn't remember the last time her mother went anywhere on her own. She never left the house except to go with Jennifer on some errand about ice skating, or with Mr. Smallwood when he was home. Her dark-blue Mercedes-Benz just sat in the garage unused.

"Isn't this lovely, Jennifer? We're making peach preserves from our orchard, the same way people in Colonial times did. The germs have all been killed by the high boiling temperatures, so we don't need artificial preservatives."

"I know, Mom. Could I have some? I'm hungry."

"Here's the pot," said Mrs. Smith. She set it on a towel on the kitchen table and smiled. "You can scrape out what's left in the bottom."

" And here's the bread we made this morning. Everything's just like the children used to do hundreds of years ago," added Lorraine Smallwood.

Jennifer took a slice of the thick bread and used a sterling silver spoon to scrape out the warm mixture and spread it onto the bread. She took a bite. "It's delicious."

"Here's some soup to go with it." Mrs. Smith brought homemade vegetable soup in a china dish along with a glass of water and more silverware.

"Jennifer," said Mrs. Smallwood, "after you eat, we're driving into Washington to fit you for a new skating costume."

Jennifer put down her spoon. "A new one? Mom, I already have dozens of costumes."

"But everyone has seen them. You need something to go with your new music and routine. I talked to Jacques on the phone and he told me what he wants."

Jennifer pushed away from the table. "I'm not hungry any more."

"Go on upstairs and change clothes," said her mother. "We leave as soon as Victor has the car ready."

Jennifer muttered under her breath. Then she took her skate case up to her room and changed into blue jeans and tee shirt, frowning into her mirror almost the whole time.

Just how many costumes did she need, anyway?

• • •

Cindy woke up just after twelve noon. Amanda was on the floor playing the Sega.

"'Bout time," said Amanda. "I'm starved."

Cindy yawned and spoke in a near-whisper. "You can eat without me."

"I wanted to cook you an omelet like my mother taught me."

Cindy pushed herself to a sitting position and yawned again. "Sounds good. Let's go."

Shortly they were up in the kitchen and Amanda was scrambling eggs along with some chopped onions and green peppers. Cindy made

toast. Finally they sat at the small dining table and Cindy took her first
bite.

"How is it?" asked Amanda.

"Uhh–it's good. Yes, it's really, really good. But, well, why is it so soupy?"
Cindy watched as some liquid egg slipped through the tines of her fork and fell
onto her plate.

"Maybe I didn't cook it long enough. Want to scrape it back into the pan?"

"No, that's okay, it's great this way." Cindy spread some of the soggy mixture onto her toast and bit in.

They drank orange juice and rinsed their dishes when they were done,
placing them in the partially-full dishwasher. Amanda scrubbed the pan she
had cooked in. Next Cindy had to do some chores: she had to empty all the
house wastebaskets into the big kitchen garbage can. She had to find and carry
all her dirty clothes down to the basement laundry room and do a load of white
stuff. Then she had to straighten up the other part of the basement from the
night before. Amanda helped so Cindy could finish faster; finally, at about one-
thirty, they were done.

Amanda put on a pink tee shirt and blue jean shorts. Cindy put on jeans
and another blue tank top. She had to tie the same dirty bandanas around her
upper arms. "I'm going to wash these things tonight; they are really yucky."
She put her door key into her pocket. They had their inline skates and protective
gear, and were about to take it all to the front stoop, when Cindy remembered
one more chore. "I have to get out some meat to thaw for supper." She ran back
to the kitchen and took a package of frozen ground meat out of the freezer. She
put it on a saucer beside the sink, then ran to the door again. "Now we can
leave."

They sat on the stoop to strap on their helmets and lace up their skates.

"Did it rain last night?" wondered Amanda.

"Pavement looks a little damp in the shadows but the sun's plenty bright, so
everything should be dry enough."

They followed the sidewalk to Turnberry and turned left, toward downtown
Murrayville. "When we come back, let's go to the library," said Cindy.

Amanda glanced back across Turnberry Avenue to the beige stucco building just visible behind the line of trees. "Sounds good."

They skated past Grace Church, which sat on the opposite side of the street,
then five blocks past other streets and houses, slightly uphill and curving left

all the way. Amanda was always just ahead of Cindy, who tried to catch up but could never quite make it. The sixth block leveled out; they raced to its end and stopped, panting, at the street light where Turnberry crossed Leslie Lane. This was the beginning of Murrayville's "downtown." Little strip malls dotted two sides of the street, with a doctor's office and a gas station on the other corners.

They waited for the light and kept following a now level Turnberry to the front of the municipal building, which also held the courthouse and post office. They crossed to the other side of the street and passed a drug store, a dress shop, an old movie theater and an ice cream parlor. The theater was going to close soon because it couldn't compete with the multiplex cinema over in Fern Oak. They bought cones in the ice cream shop and sat outside at a tiny round table to eat them.

Cones finished, they skated up Turnberry to the city park, where they raced each other along the walking paths, giving wide berth to people walking their dogs. They cut through the trees and around the duck pond, scaring the ducks. They stopped by the new skate park, a concrete bowl where boys on skateboards and inlines performed stunts that looked as if they were trying to kill themselves.

A red-haired boy motioned them in. "Come on, show us what you can do!"

Cindy hooted. "Fat chance, Kyle, you know we're better than you!"

"We don't want to make you guys look bad," Amanda shouted back.

"Oh, yeah? Race you around the park, if you think you can beat me."

So they were back on the sidewalk again, three of them this time, and the people on bicycles or walking their dogs got out of the way when they came by. Amanda got back to the skate park first. Cindy was next and Kyle last. Amanda flopped onto a park bench. The others followed suit.

"I'll beat you next time," panted Kyle. He was soaking wet from head to toe and his face was as bright as his hair, though a different shade of red.

Eventually the girls cooled off and decided to go back home. Amanda wiped her face on her pink shirt and Cindy used one of her bandanas, already so wet and salty her face seemed even damper afterward.

They crossed to the other side of Turnberry, where the clock in the courthouse read almost five. At the slope a little past Leslie Street, they squatted over their skates and let gravity pull them down faster and faster. They dug in their brakes and came to a stop just before Cedar Terrace.

"Race you to Smallwood Lane!" challenged Cindy.

• • •

After leaving her practice costume and tights on the bed for Mrs. Smith to wash, Jennifer went downstairs and joined her mother in that suffocating car.

She dozed in the back seat while Victor drove them to the outskirts of Washington, D.C., where she tried on the new costume. The costume was of expensive red velvet and she didn't like it. But Mrs. Smallwood and the dressmaker kept telling her how pretty she looked in it. Finally they were done, and Jennifer fell asleep again on the way home.

They got back an hour before suppertime. Her mother said, "Why don't you go upstairs and finish your nap?"

"All right."

But when she got to her room, Jennifer felt restless and didn't want to lie down. She stood by the window and gazed out at the afternoon of a beautiful summer day. Below her window at the back of the house was a thick green lawn surrounded by hedges, tall trees, and a flower garden. The peach orchard was just beyond the hedges. In the past, maybe fifty or a hundred years earlier, people came to this house all the time to play croquet and drink lemonade in the shade of the huge maple trees. Jennifer hadn't played in her own back yard in years.

She took off her blue jeans and put on some denim shorts, white socks, and running shoes. Then she brushed her hair back and tied it into a pony tail. She slipped her door key into her pocket, and quietly went down the front stairs, watching out for the housekeeper or anyone else who might come through.

She couldn't go out the back door because she would have to pass by her mother, who oversaw the preparation of every meal. Very carefully, Jennifer opened the front door, slipped outside, and closed it behind her. She stood on the wide, columned porch and looked all around. No one was in sight.

Quickly she descended the porch steps and walked on the damp grass, avoiding the driveway so that her shoes would not make a crunching sound. She cut across the big lawn and disappeared into the trees between the house and Smallwood Lane.

She decided not to walk along Smallwood Lane because Victor might look there for her. She kept going through the peach orchard in the direction, she hoped, of Turnberry. After awhile there were no more peach trees, and she was in the wooded area that separated the other houses from the library.

That was when it got weird.

She was getting close to Turnberry when she saw a shadowy shape ahead of her. She slowed down and ducked behind a tree, thinking it might be someone from her house, searching for her. Then the figure moved into a ray of sunlight, and Jennifer saw that it was a woman she did not know. Jennifer assumed she lived in one of the houses nearby.

Jennifer crept sideways, planning to sneak wide and avoid her. But the woman turned and smiled, and Jennifer stopped again.

"Hello." The woman was wearing a blue dress and matching high heels. The shoes caused Jennifer to wonder, because they were not easy to walk in through fallen branches and undergrowth.

"Hi," Jennifer answered automatically. She was only thinking about getting away. Then she noticed the woman's bright green eyes, pale and glowing like a jewel.

"Taking a walk through the woods?" the woman asked.

"Um, yes." Jennifer couldn't stop staring at her.

"I wonder if you might have seen my dog? I seem to have lost her. She's very small, white and fluffy. She's what's called a peek-a-poo. That's a mixture of Pekingese and poodle."

Jennifer had to think a moment. "No, I—I haven't seen any animals except squirrels."

The woman nodded. Her hair gleamed goldish-red, her eyes sea-green. "I understand you're a really good ice skater, Jennifer."

Now Jennifer was really startled. Then she decided the lady must have read about her in the sports section of the paper. "Yeah, I guess." Jennifer didn't want to talk about it.

"Have you ever roller skated?"

"Not since I was little."

"You might want to try it sometime. It's a lot of fun."

"Okay, sure."

"I have to go now."

"Bye."

The woman took a couple of steps, and then she was gone.

She just disappeared, kind of faded quickly away. She was there, and then she wasn't.

Jennifer gaped at the spot where the lady had stood outlined in the sun. There was nothing around but trees.

Then Jennifer did take a wide path around the spot.

She ran all the way to Turnberry and stopped to catch her breath. Across the street two girls raced each other along the sidewalk, the same girls she saw rollerblading all the time. They came to a halt at the corner to rest.

She wondered whether she would have had the courage to speak to them if she hadn't been so frightened.

• • •

The girls crossed Cedar Terrace, pushing as hard as they could, neither able to get ahead of the other. Finally, where Smallwood Lane cut into Evergreen Woods, they stopped and fell to the grass, out of breath and streaming with perspiration. They took off their helmets and laughed until they had cooled off.

Amanda sat up. "Who's that?"

Cindy immediately thought of Mary Jo, the skater who had supposedly died in a car wreck. She sat up quickly and looked around. "Who? I don't see anybody."

"Across the street." Amanda dipped her head to indicate the direction, and Cindy squinted slightly.

"That looks like the girl from the white Cadillac."

"It is! It's Jennifer Smallwood! She's just standing there, staring at us."

"Wow, her face really looks white."

The unsmiling girl looked both ways and crossed the street. Cindy and Amanda gaped at her coming toward them. When she reached their side, she mounted the curb and stood on the sidewalk before them. A sheen of perspiration filmed her pale face.

"Hi," said Cindy and Amanda in unison.

"Hello," the girl answered solemnly. "Do you live around here?"

"In Cedar Terrace." Amanda waved toward the townhouse development three blocks away.

"I'm Jennifer Smallwood."

"I'm Cindy Buford."

"And I'm Amanda Carter."

"It's nice to meet you."

"You, too."

"I saw something very strange," said Jennifer.

"Strange?"

"A woman. She was in the woods near my house."

Cindy's eyes grew wide. "What did she look like?"

"She had puffy light reddish hair, and she was wearing high heels. In the woods!"

Cindy and Amanda stared at each other. "Did she say anything?" asked Amanda.

"She asked me to look for her dog. Then she called me by my name and said I was a good ice skater, but I should try roller skating."

Chapter 5
New Friends

Now they were in Cindy's kitchen drinking punch.

"Well, I'm the only one who hasn't seen her," said Amanda.

"You don't want to see her," shuddered Jennifer.

"I wasn't frightened when she spoke to me. Just later, when I found out she was dead."

"Wait a minute," said Amanda, "how do you know she's dead? That old man may have been playing a trick on us. And how can you be sure that lady in the picture was the same one you saw? Maybe she just looked like her."

"What was her name again?" asked Jennifer.

"Mary Jo. That's what she told me, and the people at the skating rink said that was the name of the woman in the poster who looked like her. Her full name was Mary Jo Green. The announcer said she died last year."

"Can't you check stuff like that at the library?" asked Amanda.

Cindy jumped to her feet. "You're right! Let's go."

Jennifer looked at the kitchen wall clock, then hung her head. "It's close to six o'clock. I've been gone an hour already. My mother will be calling me to supper soon."

"Mine too," said Amanda.

"And mine will be getting home from work soon," added Cindy.

"If you're going to get into trouble," said Amanda, "maybe you'd better go home now."

"Right." Jennifer rose and then wrapped her arms around herself. "But not back through those woods."

"We'll walk you home," offered Cindy.

They ran along Turnberry back to the intersection, then crossed left and followed Smallwood. Several blocks later, when they reached the long driveway to Smallwood Mansion, they were hot and winded, and the white Cadillac was pulling up the gravel drive and just reaching the street.

"That's our chauffeur," muttered Jennifer.

The car stopped and the gray-haired man got out. He was taller when he stood up than he looked inside the car. "Your mother is worried about you," he said, though he didn't seem concerned. In fact, he was smiling.

"Is she mad?"

"Very upset. She's about to call the police."

"Oh, no," groaned all three girls at once.

"I'll drive you back to the house." He opened the back door of the car, and seemed surprised when all three girls piled in. But he closed the door and slid behind the wheel without speaking, then made a U-turn. Cindy felt a sudden chill as the air conditioning blew across her sweaty arms.

She and Amanda rubbed the smooth white leather seats and made weird faces at each other. Amanda, in the middle, pulled on a small round handle set into the back of the front seat. It opened to reveal a big ash tray, cigarette lighter, a glass and a bottle of liquor. Amanda clapped her hand over her mouth and closed it again.

Cindy played with the knobs on the armrest by her window seat. Lights came on, music started playing, and the window rolled down. Embarrassed, she fiddled with the knobs until everything was back to normal. Jennifer sat and watched them explore the car, a slight smile on her face.

The luxurious car passed through a lane of trees that seemed to go on for miles. Finally a colonial mansion came into view and the driveway circled in front of it. The car pulled around and stopped in front of the house. A tall woman who looked like Jennifer, with blonde hair in a bun high on her head, came down the steps in tears. Jennifer sighed and got out of the car to meet her. Cindy and Amanda followed.

"Oh, Jennifer! What happened to you! Where were you?"

"I just went for a walk. I wasn't sleepy after all."

Her mother hugged her. "But you should have told me. You know how much I worry about you."

"I just decided to go for a walk in the orchard. Then I reached the street, and I got to talking to a couple of friends."

Mrs. Smallwood looked sharply at Amanda and Cindy, seeming to see them for the first time. "Who are these girls?"

"They live around here, on Cedar Terrace. Amanda Carter, Cindy Buford, this is my mother, Mrs. Smallwood."

"Pleased to meet you," said Mrs. Smallwood, although she looked anything but. "Would you like to come inside?"

Cindy and Amanda glanced at each other, then at Mrs. Smallwood's unsmiling face.

"Um, we have to get home too, our mothers might wonder where we are," said Cindy.

"Right." Amanda nodded vigorously. "Yeah, we have to go. Nice to meet you. 'Bye, Jennifer." Amanda backed around the car toward the driveway. Cindy followed, glancing back several times to smile at the Smallwoods.

Jennifer said, "But you're still going with me tomorrow, right?"

They stopped. "Tomorrow?"

"To watch me ice skate, like we said." Jennifer looked seriously at her mother. "They're very good roller skaters, and I think they could be good ice skaters."

Mrs. Smallwood's eyes were wide and puzzled. "I—well, of course, they can go with you if they'd like. They'll just have to get up rather early."

"I don't have ballet on Tuesdays. We can pick them up at 9:00. Right, Victor?"

Victor's face broke out in an amused grin. "Whatever you say, Boss."

Cindy got a sudden idea. "And you're coming to the roller rink with us for the Wednesday afternoon session, right?"

"Yes, I'd love to." Jennifer looked sideways at her mother. "Do you think I might skip my lesson Wednesday morning? I can't do both kinds of skating in the same day."

Mrs. Smallwood scowled. "We'll have to have a discussion about that."

She nodded at her daughter's departing friends. "Nice to have met you both. Come back any time." Then she pursed her lips.

"Sure. Bye!"

The two girls walked, then jogged, down the long driveway, looking back frequently to wave at the shrinking figures observing their escape.

•••

Mrs. Smallwood guided her daughter inside. "I don't know what's gotten into you, leaving like that without telling me. And those girls! They look . . ." She paused and took a short, sniffing breath. "Well, you shouldn't have run off like that."

Jennifer could imagine what her mother was thinking: that the two girls probably didn't have much money, but Mrs. Smallwood would never allow herself to appear snobbish by running them down because they were poor.

Outwardly Jennifer kept her face solemn, but secretly she was smiling. Victor shook his head and, still grinning, drove the car around to the garage.

•••

Cindy and Amanda were out of breath and had to stop running long before they reached the lane. By Cedar Terrace they were ready to drop.

"My mother's probably wondering where I am," said Amanda.

"Mine'll be home soon, but I'll go with you and we'll explain what happened."

Mrs. Carter seemed angry and worried. "You got into a strange car and went to a strange house?" she demanded.

The girls looked at each other. "We never thought about it," said Amanda. "We see her and her white car all the time on the street."

"So do I, but I wouldn't get in with them."

"Well—she's taking us ice skating tomorrow. She's picking us up at Cindy's house." Amanda paused. "If it's okay with you, I mean."

Her mother frowned in concern. "I have to be certain that's where she and her chauffeur are actually taking you both. We don't know these people."

"Why don't you wait with us at my house," asked Cindy, "and give the chauffeur the third degree?"

"Yeah. Scare the britches off him so he'll be afraid to molest us."

"Amanda! Now I think I'm going to say you can't go."

"Oh, please, Mom!"

"Please, Mrs. Carter!"

"Well, we'll see. Amanda, please go inside and set the table for supper. Cindy, I'll talk to you in the morning."

Cindy and Amanda grimaced at each other. As Cindy was leaving she said, "Later tonight, if my mom'll let me, I'm going to go to the library."

"Darn, I wanted to come. Call me later and tell me what you find out."

"Okay."

Cindy got home just before her mother walked in the door. Mrs. Buford's face was slick with sweat because her car's air conditioning didn't work. She wasn't in a very good mood.

"Oh, Cindy, those bandannas on your arms are dripping wet and they look terrible."

Cindy began trying to untie the pieces of cloth, but the bandannas were so wet and the knots so tight that she gave up and began trying to pull them down her arms. It was difficult to get them over her elbows.

"Did you thaw out that package of hamburger?" asked Mrs. Buford..

"Huh? Umm–yes."

"Good. I'll cook supper. You can set the table and bring up the clean laundry. But wash your sweaty hands first." Mrs. Buford put her purse on the shelf in the coat closet, kicked off her white high-heeled sandals, and walked into the kitchen.

Cindy followed her. "Mom, after supper, could I go to the library?"

Mrs. Buford scowled at her daughter. "You couldn't go earlier today?"

"I was busy."

"Well, we'll see. It's dangerous to go out after dark."

"Mom, I'm twelve years old and it won't be dark for a couple of hours!"

• • •

Inside the library, Cindy walked past tables with children and adults, and many shelves of books, to reach a long row of desks holding computer terminals. She accessed the library's search engine, followed the instructions for finding people, and then typed in "Mary Jo Green."

A message appeared. "There are seven hundred newspaper articles and web stories on the subject of 'Mary Jo Green.'"

Where had she lived? Fern Oak? Murrayville? She typed "Mary Jo Green, Fern Oak, Maryland."

That brought nothing. She tried again, changing "Fern Oak" to "Murrayville." Twenty entries appeared.

There were ten articles on roller skating competitions; Mary Jo Green's name was listed along with other people who had won medals. There were three articles about charity races where she had raised money by running. She had won some awards for being the year's top salesperson of La Belle cosmetics. She had also won an award at the travel agency where she'd worked.

And, there was her obituary.

Cindy kept reading its words over and over. After a while she logged off the computer and thanked the librarian. She ran all the way home, hardly able to wait until she could call Amanda and tell her what she'd found out.

●●●

In Smallwood Mansion, Jennifer searched the net with her computer, using the keywords "Mary Jo Green." After she had eliminated all the people with the same and similar names, she sat frowning at the information on the screen.

"I don't believe it. It's a hoax. That doesn't even look like the woman I saw." She shut down the computer and went to bed.

●●●

Amanda asked to use her father's PC. It took her awhile, but she learned some startling news. She was still trying to understand it when the phone rang.

"Amanda," called her mother, "it's for you."

Amanda went to the phone. Cindy was on the other end.

"You'll never guess what!" Cindy gasped. "That lady, that Mary Jo Green? She was—" Cindy paused for breath.

"No, I already know! She was—"

"Mary Jo Green used to live in Evergreen Woods. And she was the woman who was killed in that hit-and-run accident at the corner of Turnberry and Smallwood!"

Chapter 6
The Ice Rink

The girls were waiting on the doorstep when the white Cadillac arrived at Cindy's house on Tuesday morning. Mrs. Carter and Amanda's little brother Tayvon, were waiting in the van. When Jennifer got out of the car, Cindy was surprised at how much she acted like a "young lady," the way Cindy was always being urged by her own mother to act. Jennifer politely introduced herself and the chauffeur to Mrs. Carter and Tayvon. Then she invited everyone to get in.

Cindy thought Mrs. Carter looked very nice in her shorts and tee shirt. Their green color was bright against her dark brown legs and arms. "I'm going to follow in my van," she said. "I might want to do some shopping after we leave the ice rink."

Cindy heard Amanda groan with embarrassment. It was obvious to everyone that Mrs. Carter didn't really trust the rich people.

Cindy and Amanda climbed inside the back seat of the huge white car, Jennifer next to them. The leather seats were just as comfortable as Cindy remembered. The Cadillac started for Fern Oak and The Ice House, while Mrs. Carter and Tayvon followed in the blue van.

When the car stopped, the chauffeur held the doors for the girls and then opened the trunk to take out a rolling pilot's bag, which he wheeled over to Jennifer. He waited with the car while the three girls walked inside, Jennifer pulling the pilot's bag. Mrs. Carter parked the van the next space over and followed with Tayvon.

They walked through the lobby, past the pro shop and the admissions desk, and pushed through some double doors into the rink proper, where they got a real shot of cold air. Jennifer went to change clothes for her lesson; Mrs. Carter and Tayvon passed along the barrier that surrounded the ice and went to wait in the refreshment area. The barrier was made of wood from the ground up to about waist height, then topped by plexiglass for a long way up.

Cindy and Amanda got tan skates from the skate rental shop that sat in a big alcove near the double doors. The rental ice skates were even uglier than those at the roller rink. They had both worn jeans and tee shirts; now they pulled on sweatshirts, Amanda's pink, Cindy's an old red one. They sat on a wooden bench to lace up their boots. Then they walked clumsily across the textured plastic floor, unable to roll like they would have in their in-line skates. Amanda's left ankle kept buckling inward. "It's these boots!" she said. "They don't give support like roller blades. And they hurt!"

"They are not comfortable" answered Cindy. Amanda was right: inline roller boots had such firm sides she could hardly bend her ankles in them, while these ice rentals were made of flimsy, unlined leather that rubbed through Cindy's thin socks and let her ankles sag inward.

They reached the barrer, where they could see Jennifer skating in a white warm-up suit that had a colorful logo on the back of the jacket. She stopped, came to the gate, and opened the door onto the ice to talk to them.

"There are only supposed to be private lessons on the ice right now," she told them, "but I talked my mother into letting me pay for some ice time for you. Just stay down at the far end if you can, out of everyone's way." She looked at their hands. "Didn't you bring any gloves?"

"Um, I guess we forgot," said Amanda. She looked sideways at Cindy, who just nodded.

"I'm sorry, I don't have any extras with me. I have to go take my lesson now." Jennifer glided off toward a man in tight black clothes who waited in the center. The man smiled and began instructing her.

Cindy surveyed the good ice skaters, five or six including Jennifer. They whizzed around the ice, cutting in and out, sometimes barely avoiding each other. "It looks more dangerous than the skatepark."

"I don't think I want to go out there."

"Oh, well, come on," said Cindy. "She paid for it, so let's skate."

They stepped onto the ice, held the wall, and moved toward the far end of the rink. It was slippery, clumsy going because of the awful, cheap skates. Accomplished skaters streaked past doing jumps and spins, performing intricate footwork. A couple of them were young children. Cindy felt embarrassed.

Jennifer was doing a spin, her back arched, one hand grasping her free ankle and holding that foot to the back of her head.

Cindy stopped and gaped. For a few moments, Jennifer spun so fast she blurred. Then in one fluid motion she let go and lowered the foot, crossed it over the other one at the ankle, and finished in a "scratch" spin. Cindy knew that from watching skating championships on TV.

The coach said something to Jennifer, and she began to practice jumps. Cindy recognized two of them from television. Using a backward cross-foot motion Jennifer gained speed, then turned, stepped forward, and leapt, rising and revolving several times before gracefully landing backward on one foot. Cindy knew that was an Axel. For the next jump Jennifer stuck one leg straight behind her and drove her toepick into the ice, then sprang high into the air to twirl several times before landing. And that was a Lutz.

Then Jennifer did some jumps that Cindy didn't recognize. Cindy liked the way Jennifer kept a confident smile on her face the whole time, even when she fell once. Cindy had watched many ice skating championships on TV, and thought Jennifer looked as good as any of the champions who had won gold medals over the years.

Cindy was about halfway down the rink; Amanda was next to her. She began shuffling along and finally reached the far end. It was getting a little easier to move on the ice.

Jennifer's coach apparently began instructing Jennifer in one particular jump, because the blond-haired girl had to keep doing it over and over. That got boring, so Cindy started watching the other skaters.

A little girl was practicing a two-foot spin nearby. Amanda tried to copy her and fell onto the ice with a shriek. Cindy skated over and extended a hand, but lost her own balance and fell flat. When she tried to push to her feet the ice was so cold on her bare hands that she yanked them into the air and fell again.

Jennifer stopped beside them with a twist of her blades. She bent over and held out a hand to help them up. "Are you two all right?"

"We're fine," Amanda answered, smiling. "We can get up on our own."

Cindy stared down at the ice; she was not feeling very fine right then.

Jennifer went back to her lesson. Cindy and Amanda crossed the couple of feet to the wall on their elbows and knees and hauled themselves up grimacing. "My hands are freezing and my butt hurts," complained Cindy. She stuck her hands under her sweatshirt and inside her underarms and stood against the wall, shivering.

Amanda tried blowing on her own palms.

"Does that help?" asked Cindy.

"Not much."

They stood in the icy cold while others performed amazing feats. Cindy wanted to go hide.

"Shall we get off the ice?" she asked.

"Not me. I'm going to learn this." Amanda pulled herself around the end of the rink, along the wall. After about ten feet, she turned and started back, this time moving her feet to help.

Cindy glared at the expert show-offs. "I wish I were at home," she muttered. Then she began to copy Amanda, using the same method of propulsion and with about as much grace.

Soon they took a break and left the ice by an exit close to the snack bar. They drank hot chocolate with Tayvon and Mrs. Carter. Tayvon kept sucking hot chocolate up into his tiny straw and blowing it at Amanda. Amanda kept telling him to stop. Mrs. Carter finally took his cup away from him. "If you're not going to drink it, then you don't need it," she informed him. She took the styrofoam cup and dropped it into the trash.

They went back to the ice and kept trying. They saw that Jennifer had finished her lesson and was practicing what she had learned. They left the ice again and stood behind the wall to watch. By the time Jennifer left the ice, Cindy and Amanda had already turned in their rental skates.

Jennifer took off her own smooth beige skates and wiped the blades with a towel before putting them into their case. She went to the ladies' room and changed back into her white shorts and blouse. Then all three girls went outside, followed by Amanda's mother and brother. The sun felt good, and the hot leather seats of the Cadillac were more comfortable than any sofa Cindy had ever sat on. They left the windows down and let the balmy noontime air warm them while Victor drove them back to Cedar Terrace. Mrs. Carter and Tayvon were again driving behind.

Victor let them out in front of Amanda's house. Cindy asked, "You're coming roller skating with us tomorrow afternoon, right?"

"Right." Jennifer smiled in what Cindy thought was a defiant expression as she waved goodbye. The limousine went up to a side street to turn around. Mrs. Carter pulled the van into the townhouse's assigned parking space.

The two girls used the handrail going up Amanda's front steps; their legs were stiff and aching. Inside, they collapsed onto the floor of the tiny foyer. Tayvon followed and danced around, laughing at them.

"Are we ever going to do that again?" asked Amanda.

"I'm not," answered Cindy.

Mrs. Carter entered and closed the front door. "Get up, girls, we have to fix lunch." She went on past them into the kitchen.

Tayvon stayed, hopping from one foot to the other and giggling.

• • •

Jennifer rode in the back seat and smiled to herself all the way back to her house. Inside, she carried her skates up to her room and put them into her closet. Then she went to stand in front of her mirror and brush her hair.

She was smiling. Really, actually smiling. She had enjoyed her lesson for the first time in a long time. She knew it was because she had friends there with her, even though they were not good skaters.

She stopped and reflected on that thought. Well, did she have any friends who ice skated? Or in her ballet class? Or at school? She didn't dislike any of the girls she associated with all the time. She just didn't feel close to them. It was as if they were too much like her. No, wait, that wasn't true. Lots of those girls weren't rich. They didn't have chauffeurs. Their parents had to work hard to pay for their lessons and for school. So how were those girls different from Amanda and Cindy?

It puzzled Jennifer as she went downstairs to eat lunch. She was so preoccupied that she didn't even worry about her mother giving her icy looks from across the table. When she was almost finished eating, she realized what the reason was.

It was because the three girls shared a secret that they couldn't tell the grown-ups about.

There was a ghost in the neighborhood who had spoken only to them. Who would believe a thing like that?

On the other hand . . .

Jennifer shuddered. She wasn't sure she believed it either.

•••

During lunch Mrs. Carter said to Amanda, "We have to finish unpacking the rest of the boxes. We're having that party for your dad's office on Friday."

There were boxes sitting everywhere, all over the house. Each day the Carters unpacked at least one container and put away the things inside.

Amanda groaned, "Mom, I'm so tired."

"Rest awhile and eat. You'll feel okay soon."

Actually, the place was getting better. Nothing obstructed the hallway any more. The worst spots were in the yellow kitchen, though it only had two packages. One was blocking the yellow counter, making it hard to prepare food. A bigger one sat under the table, getting in the way of the kitchen chairs and anybody sitting in them. Cindy and Amanda had to keep their feet wrapped around their chair legs while they ate soup and lunchmeat sandwiches. Tayvon folded his legs under himself and chortled under his breath as he kept pouring soup from his spoon into his bowl. Mrs. Carter stood at the counter to eat.

Amanda thought about the work to be done. Up in her pink bedroom the containers had been emptied and everything put away; the same with Tayvon's blue bedroom. Amanda had done most of the work in both rooms. She'd helped her Mom put away stuff in the white bathrooms, upstairs and downstairs, and her mom and dad had pretty much finished with their own green bedroom.

"Mom, we don't have to get the basement ready too, do we?"

A big mess remained downstairs in the basement/family room, where boxes were stacked to the ceiling, furniture was piled loveseat on game table on sofa, and curtains didn't yet cover the two windows or the sliding glass doors into the enclosed back garden.

"No, we're leaving that till later. Hopefully everyone will fit into the living room."

After they were finished eating, Amanda said, "Come on, let's get started." She led Cindy back to the living room, directly behind the kitchen.

The elegant gold and brown furniture was arranged just so on the brown shag carpet. The gold curtains across the back picture window were carefully hung, while the light wooden end tables, dining room set, and bookshelves all shone with polish. Cindy and Amanda took decorative items from their boxes and arranged them on shelves and display cases.

The whole time, they talked about things that had been going on recently.

"Jennifer's pretty good," Amanda commented.

"Yep. I guess she has good reason to be stuck on herself."

"But she's not really like that. She's actually pretty friendly. Anyway, there's never a good reason for somebody to act better than anybody else."

Amanda leaned close then and whispered something into Cindy's ear. "And I bet Mary Jo Green would say the same thing." They had agreed to keep quiet around their parents about meeting a dead person. Mrs. Carter was still in the kitchen and might overhear them.

Cindy whispered back, "You don't know what Mary Jo would say. You haven't met her yet, remember?"

Amanda didn't answer. As she ran the vacuum cleaner over the rug, she wondered if she ever would see the ghost.

Chapter 7
The Roller Rink Again

At twelve-thirty on Wednesday afternoon, the Cadillac arrived at Amanda's doorstep. Jennifer did not look very happy when she got out of the back and said, "My mom won't let me go in your van. I have to ride with Victor." Jennifer gave her chauffeur a hostile sideways look, but he ignored it and smiled at everyone. Mrs. Carter nodded in understanding.

"So can we ride with you again?" asked Cindy.

"Sure," Jennifer answered. They all got into the back.

At the rink, Mrs. Carter sat in the refreshment area reading a book while the three girls and Tayvon skated. There was one party table of kids about nine years old, so there weren't just really little kids and their parents to dodge this time. Amanda, dressed in pink shorts and shirt, was mortified because she had to hold her little brother's hand and keep him from falling. He didn't want to go any faster than a snail's pace. Cindy skated slowly beside them in her blue tank top and denim shorts with the bandannas around her arms. The girls' legs began to hurt as their hip muscles tightened up from skating at a snail's pace. "Go sit down with Mom," Amanda griped and tried to extricate her hand from Tayvon's. "Stop bugging me."

"No! I wanna skate!"

He squeezed tighter and yanked on her arm so hard they both almost fell. In retaliation she struck out into the middle of the floor, skating so fast he yelled in fear. They circled the rink a couple of times, her dragging him along and him yelling. Cindy glanced to where Mrs. Carter was sitting. She was ignoring them.

Finally both Amanda and Tayvon calmed down. He held his feet still and parallel and let her pull him along at a reasonable speed. By then he was smiling happily.

Cindy wondered if she would have to put up with the same type of behavior from her little brother when he got a few years older. She remembered the fighting she'd seen between older and younger brothers and sisters back in her old neighborhood. Probably the future held the same for her and Peter.

Mrs. Carter continued acting as if she wasn't aware of anything, although Cindy saw her peek their way a couple of times, then turn back to her book.

Jennifer wore white clothes and very expensive inline roller skates. "My father gave them to me for Christmas. My mom was really mad. He doesn't think I should spend all my time ice skating, but he's hardly ever around." She was having difficulty adjusting to wheels instead of metal blades, but she was doing better than Cindy and Amanda had on ice the day before.

After a while she began trying ice moves, jumps and arabesques, though she wasn't able to spin. The floor was crowded with kids going every direction, so she had to be cautious. Often other skaters would cut in front of her. When she frowned at them, Cindy noticed that Jennifer looked very much like Mrs. Smallwood.

Not to be outdone, Cindy tried skating the way she had the Saturday before at the end of the session, but there were too many kids.

Then the games started. They joined in, but younger kids always won. In addition to the games, there were racing contests.

The races were divided into age groups. First were little kids up to five years old. Tayvon wanted to enter that group, but his mother said he wasn't good enough. At that Amanda stuck her tongue out at him.

Next were not so little ones six to nine. None of the racers could go very fast, despite cheering and clapping from their friends and families.

Then came the race for ten to twelve-year-olds. Cindy, Amanda, and Jennifer were the only ones in that group. They lined up at a black mark painted across one side of the floor; the referee was the same floor guard from before.

He blew the whistle and they took off racing down the floor and around the corners. Mrs. Carter and Tayvon and some of the other kids cheered them on. The race wasn't long enough; they had only circled two laps when Amanda crossed the finish line first and the referee blew his whistle. Cindy was next, and Jennifer just behind her. Amanda won a certificate for a slice of pizza.

A couples skate was next. Tayvon sat with his mother while the three girls bought sodas. Cindy and Jennifer had to buy their own pizza; Amanda was hungry and ate all of her prize piece.

The gray-haired lady with the long braid was behind the snack bar. Cindy asked her, "Where's Barbara?"

"She'll be here later."

Cindy took Jennifer to the wall posters. "See anyone familiar?"

Jennifer shook her head. "I don't follow roller skating." Then she gasped and pointed to the picture of Mary Jo Green in her shiny pink, bejeweled costume. "That's the woman in the woods!"

Cindy nodded. "That's Mary Jo Green."

Jennifer's face went white, the way it had been the day they'd met her. "No, it must have been someone else. Mary Jo Green is dead."

Cindy opened her mouth to speak, but Jennifer skated away and drank her soda by herself in the last booth.

Shortly before the session ended, Barbara McAllister came in carrying full plastic bags. Cindy pulled Jennifer to where Barbara was taking cleaning supplies from the bags and putting them into a closet beside the men's restroom. Amanda came and joined them, for once without Tayvon.

"Hello."

Barbara McAllister looked around and smiled. "Oh, hi. Back to entertain us again?"

Cindy said, "This is my friend, Jennifer Smallwood. She's an ice skater. Mary Jo Green talked to her, too, didn't she, Jennifer?"

Barbara's face lost its smile. She turned back to the grocery bags.

"I can't be sure of that," Jennifer objected. "I saw a lady in the woods who looked like that picture, that's all."

Amanda said excitedly, "Is it true that Mary Jo was in a hit-and-run accident at the corner of Smallwood and Turnberry last year? We all live near that intersection." Beside her, Jennifer looked uncomfortable.

Barbara sighed. "I really don't think this is a funny game."

"Look, we're not playing. We just want to know how she died."

Barbara considered, then apparently decided to answer them. "I don't know anything except that she died in Murrayville, not far from where she lived." Barbara abruptly closed the door, and locked it with a key from a huge brass keyring. "If you'll excuse me, I have people coming for skating practice."

Jennifer spoke. "Skating practice?"

Barbara's manner became more businesslike. "Club members have to get ready for the National Roller Skating Championships in Lincoln, Nebraska, next week." Barbara nodded toward the front door. A blond-haired lady in denim shorts was coming in, followed by twin Asian girls. They wore sundress-style skating costumes in gold and black leopard print, and they were pulling black pilot cases.

"Hi, Carol!" called Barbara. "I'll be ready in just a few minutes." Barbara walked toward the office.

"Wow, maybe we can stay and watch!" exclaimed Amanda. "I'll go ask my mom." She skated toward the snack bar, where Mrs. Carter was trying to unlace Tayvon's rental skates.

Cindy and Jennifer stood at the railing to watch the twins remove white leather roller skates from their black cases. The two unlaced the skates and put them on while the woman with them came to lean on the wall near Jennifer and Cindy.

"Do you want to watch?" Cindy asked Jennifer.

The blond-haired girl nodded. "I've never seen a roller skating performance."

"Will you get in trouble with your mom?"

She shrugged. "I don't know. Probably."

Cindy wondered why Jennifer didn't seem worried.

The announcer called for the last couples skate. Most of the overhead lights went out. Then the mirrored globe lit up and began to turn, sending flashes of reflection across the walls and floor. The three girls took off their skates and went back to the railing. The lady in the denim shorts watched the remaining session skaters race or stumble around the darkened floor under the globe's flashes.

The two identical girls skated over.

"Are those your daughters?" asked Cindy, indicating the twins.

"Yes, adopted from China. Britt and Tiff are seven years old. I'm Carol Parton."

"Hi, I'm Cindy, and this is my friend Jennifer. Your daughters are really cute."

"Why, thank you." Britt and Tiff smiled shyly but didn't answer.

Cindy heard the door squeal and saw it open again. A man and woman wearing matching yellow polo shirts came in laughing and talking, pulling skate bags. They sat down to put on their skates, still joking.

Amanda came back. "My mom says we can stay for a little while."

At the door, an African-American teenaged girl entered. Dressed in a white tee shirt and black leggings, she immediately sat and began slipping her feet inside white leather skates. She was followed shortly by an African-American man who laughed and boomed "Hello!" to the club skaters. People shouted back, "Hi, Garrett!"

"Cindy," exclaimed Amanda, "all these people are in those posters!"

The girls gazed at the distant wall where the posters of skaters were hung, but they couldn't see any of the pictures clearly.

The lights came back on and the announcer directed people to remove their rental skates as the session was over. It took a while until all the parents and little kids had cleared out. By then Barbara was pushing a wide dustmop around the skating floor to clean up the dirt, candy wrappers, and other junk dropped during the session. The club skaters went onto the floor and practiced in the areas she had already finished. They were doing tricks like spins and jumps, much like what the ice skaters had been doing the day before.

More arrived at the front door, including a boy and girl whom Cindy recognized as the young poster couple dressed in red and black. Today the boy wore jeans and a black shirt while the girl had on a green striped skating costume.

Jennifer went outside to speak to Victor, then came back in. She nodded when Cindy asked her if she could stay. Jennifer, Cindy, and Amanda stood and watched. All the skaters were now out on the floor, whizzing around in every direction, and the place appeared close to pandemonium. Yet the skaters avoided each other and seemed not to worry about getting knocked down.

Cindy and Amanda made admiring comments about the many feats of grace and daring, but Jennifer was not particularly impressed. Of the teenaged girl rushing around the floor doing jumps and spins, Jennifer said, "I can do everything she's doing, and I don't fall down as much." It was true; the tall, dark girl did fall often.

Jennifer explained that the man and woman in polo shirts were doing something called team dance, exact steps in a set pattern to a prescribed tempo of music. Then she said, "Their footwork is sloppy and their speed is sluggish."

The boy and girl were practicing pairs moves. They looked about ten years old. "We have couples younger than they are," said Jennifer, "with moves stronger and faster."

In the center of the floor were some black circles painted onto the surface. The Afro-American man and the oriental girls were following the lines on one foot, doing figure eights and serpentines, sometimes with intricate turns and backward moves.

"What are they doing?" Cindy asked the girls' mother, Carol Parton.

"School figures. And Garrett is doing loop circles."

"Ice doesn't have figures any more," commented Jennifer. "Now we have 'Moves in the Field.' I actually miss doing figures. Ice figures are more graceful than those they're doing on wood."

Mrs. Parton frowned at Jennifer. Cindy was sure it was because she had heard the disparaging remarks about the other roller skaters, and didn't like Jennifer criticizing her daughters.

"I don't care how bad they are," commented Cindy, "they're all better than I am, and I wish I could do that stuff."

Jennifer scowled. "Well, I don't."

Amanda's mother came up to the railing. "Tayvon and I are tired. It's time to go, girls."

"Okay." Cindy, Amanda, and Jennifer followed Mrs. Carter out the front door.

Jennifer went to the Cadillac. "Goodbye," she called. "Thanks so much for inviting me. I'll see you soon."

"Bye," the others called back, and got into the minivan.

●●●

The drive home was taken up by discussions of roller skating champions and how unpleasant Jennifer had been.

"I'm beginning to think she really is stuck-up," stated Amanda.

"She was snobbish about the roller skaters. Like she was so much better than them."

"Well, she is better. None of the roller skaters did spins and jumps as hard as what she did yesterday. And she only fell once."

"We only saw that one girl doing spins and jumps," Amanda pointed out. "The only other people who fell were those two little kids skating pairs."

"I thought they were all wonderful," commented Mrs. Carter. "So Jennifer did a better job on ice?"

"Lots better," affirmed Amanda.

Amanda and Cindy saw they were getting close to home. They began whispering about Mary Jo Green and hit-and-run drivers.

Cindy said, "The only witness was an old lady who lived near Mary Jo's house, but I didn't write down the name or address. Maybe we could find the lady and talk to her."

"Sounds good," commented Amanda. "And this time—" she raised her eyebrows— "this time, I'm coming too."

●●●

When Jennifer Smallwood walked into her house, Mrs. Smallwood was sitting in the kitchen, reading a magazine and drinking herbal tea. *The correct term is tisane, not tea,* Jennifer reminded herself. Her mother pursed her mouth but kept reading as Jennifer laid her inline skates on the floor and went to open the refrigerator. Jennifer found an apple and sat down at the carved, dark wooden table.

Finally Mrs. Smallwood spoke. "Did you have a good time?" she asked.

Jennifer wanted to get back at her mother for not letting her ride in the van with the Carters. She chewed and swallowed a bite of apple before answering. "Yes, the roller skating was wonderful. I watched some competitive skaters practice for their national championships. They were really good, better even than some of the skaters at The Ice House."

Lorraine Smallwood made a disapproving sound. She looked directly at her daughter. Her eyes held an unyielding expression.

"I'm glad that you enjoyed yourself. Now it's time to apply yourself to ice skating. No more dallying around with other things." She turned back to the magazine as if the discussion were over.

Jennifer curiously stared at her mother. "Why not, Mom? What's wrong with a little variety now and then?"

Mrs. Smallwood didn't even bother to look up. "People who spend all their time having fun never get anywhere in life."

"When do I ever have fun?"

Now she did gaze at Jennifer. Her eyes were demanding. "Are you telling me that you don't like ice skating? Jennifer, you've such a wonderful talent! How can you even think about wasting it?"

"Not everybody is Peggy Fleming or Dorothy Hamill or even Sarah Hughes. What makes you think I'll ever win the Olympics?"

"I don't expect that of you! I just want you to–to try your best."

"And be perfect in everything I do."

Her mother nodded. "No one can reach perfection, but everyone can strive for it."

"What do you care if I'm perfect or not? You never come to the rink to watch me any more. You don't even know how my skating looks now. You just talk to Jacques by telephone and take his word for it. You used to go out by yourself all the time. Now the only time you ever leave the house is when Victor drives you to the beauty shop or you want to look at a costume for me. Is that the kind of life you want me to live too?"

Lorraine Smallwood became strangely quiet. She didn't say anything. She just stared at her daughter, yet Jennifer felt as if her mother did not see her.

"Mom?" Jennifer felt an odd twinge of apprehension.

Her mother took a deep breath. Her eyes focused on Jennifer again. "To-morrow we will take you for a second fitting of your new skating costume. And if you skip practice again, for any reason, you are going to be punished."

Jennifer tossed her head. "Fine." She stood and put her apple core into the wastebasket under the sink. As she left the kitchen, she saw her mother take a deep, shaky breath, then stare into her empty cup. Her magazine lay forgotten on the tabletop.

Jennifer went upstairs to her room, where she logged onto her computer and visited all sorts of websites of which she knew her mother would not approve.

Chapter 8
The Witness

On Thursday morning, Cindy woke up early with a stomach ache. She was moaning in her bed when her mother passed by in the hall on her way to take a shower.

"Honey, what's wrong?"

"My stomach hurts. I think it was the pizza I ate yesterday at the skating rink."

"Do you want me to stay home from work with you?"

Grimacing, Cindy shook her head. "No, I'll be okay. Amanda and I are going to the library later."

"Well, don't go anywhere if you're sick." Mrs. Buford stood. "Hon, I really have to get ready for work."

Her mom left the room, and Cindy fell in and out of a crazy doze. She kept seeing a woman with green eyes and a pink skating costume who was trying to tell her something, but Cindy couldn't make it out. Cindy woke up again when she heard her mother go out the front door and close it behind her. Then she went into a deep sleep.

She woke again to the phone's ringing. She crept across to her mom's bedroom, took the receiver from the nightstand, and lay down on her mom's bed. "Hello?"

"It's me," said Amanda's voice. "It's after ten o'clock. Do you want to go searching for Mary Jo?"

"I can't. I'm sick. Bad stomach ache. Are you sick too?"

"No, I'm fine." There was a pause. Amanda asked, "Shall I go by myself?"

"Yeah, I guess so. Tell me what you find."

"You sure you can't come?"

"Can't."

"Okay, 'Bye."

Cindy hung up the phone and fell back to sleep.

• • •

Amanda dressed in jeans and a light pink tee shirt. She was at her front door, skates slung across her shoulder, when her mother called her name.

"Amanda, where are you going?" Mrs. Carter stood at the far end of the front hall where the basement steps led down. She was holding a laundry basket. Tayvon stuck his head around the doorjamb and grinned.

"Out to skate," answered Amanda.

Her mother carried the basket toward her while Tayvon followed, giggling. "I'm sorry, I need you to help me clean house and buy groceries today. We have to get ready for the party tomorrow night."

"But this house is clean enough!" wailed Amanda.

"We all have work to do, even Tayvon."

Amanda put her hands on her hips. "What's his big important job?"

"I have to sweep the front steps and sidewalk," her brother answered proudly.

"Right," said his mother. "So take the short broom and get to work. Leave the front door open and the glass screen closed so I can see you."

Amanda helped with dusting and mopping while her little brother played outside with the toy broom that had been hers when she was his age. When she thought she was done, her mother sent her to collect bathroom linens and wash them. Mrs. Carter spent the time opening and emptying packing boxes and putting away the stuff in them.

They went to the Big Buy supermarket outside Fern Oak and spent a couple of hours buying groceries. Finally, when they got home and the groceries were all put away, her mother said she could relax for a while. It was nearly four o'clock.

"May I use Dad's computer?"

"All right, but don't play any games on it. It's just for education."

"I remember."

Amanda found the obituaries on Mary Jo Green again and printed them out. Then she went looking for on-line newspaper articles related to the accident. She found three, but none of them told her much.

The first related that Mary Jo had died the year before on Monday, July 26th at 5:30 p.m., struck down by a mysterious, dark-colored automobile as she walked her dog. The car had then sped away. The only witness was a lady named Rose Witcrest who lived on Smallwood Lane in Evergreen Woods. The next two articles repeated the facts and stated that the police had no other leads.

Amanda printed the articles, then looked around until she found the phone book. She looked up Rose Witcrest and wrote the woman's address, 3514 Smallwood Lane, and phone number on the same sheet as the most informative article. Then she tried to find Mary Jo Green's name and address on the internet, but only came up with the newspaper articles again.

By the time Amanda got downstairs, it was nearly five o'clock.

"Mom, may I go out skating for a while?"

"With Cindy?"

"No, she's sick today."

"Amanda, if you're by yourself, you'll forget what time it is and you'll be late for supper."

"No, I'm wearing my watch." She held her arm up so her mother could see the bright pink watchband with the Cinderella watch face on her left wrist.

"Well, be sure to keep looking at it. And I don't want you to cross Turnberry any more. I've heard it's a dangerous road. A neighbor told me a woman was killed there a year ago."

"Mary Jo Green."

"Who?"

"Her name was Mary Jo Green. She used to skate at the Roller Haven. She was a champion."

Her mother stared at her a moment. "That same skating rink we went to yesterday?"

"That's right."

Mrs. Carter turned away, frowning. "Yes. Well. Don't be late for supper." She began chopping lettuce for a salad.

•••

Outside the sky was overcast, but the air was heavy with the late afternoon heat that had been building all day. Sweat swelled between Amanda's cornrows and rolled down her face as she bent over her skate straps. She rose from the steps and wiped the salt from her eyes and onto her short sleeve.

She glided down the path to the sidewalk and jumped curbs until she reached Turnberry, then followed that road to Smallwood Lane and turned right into Evergreen Woods housing development. The street curved around about a half-block before the first houses appeared, some very nice single-family homes with green lawns and pastel-colored siding, some with fences in back. After another block or so the single houses were replaced by duplexes, small double houses joined together at the middle with one big yard around the two of them.

Amanda skated about two more blocks before she found Rose Witcrest's house. She made sure of the address one more time by checking the paper in her pocket. Then she skated past several times, trying to decide what to do.

Two white concrete driveways, no more than a foot's distance between them, led through neatly mown grass to the side-by-side white garage doors of the blue duplex listed as Rose Witcrest's address. The porches and front doors were on opposite ends of the building. A short, white picket fence closed off the back yard of 3514, the door on the left. The yard of the house on the right, 3512, was unenclosed.

Amanda had never walked up to strangers' houses and knocked on their doors. Well, actually, she had when she'd sold Girl Scout cookies door-to-door, but her mom and another girl had always been with her. So this was different. She was standing on the sidewalk, looking at 3514 and trying to decide what to say, when a gate in the fence opened. Startled, Amanda skated about ten feet up the sidewalk.

Through the gate came one of the strangest-looking ladies Amanda had ever seen. Not only was she extremely short, with her head barely reaching above the fence, she was also very fat, and waddled from side to side when she walked.

She was dressed like a cowgirl in a red long-sleeved shirt, of all things for a hot day in July. Long white fringe swung from the sleeves, hem, and pockets. Below that was a blue denim gathered skirt. On the lady's feet, extending almost up to her short knees, were white cowboy boots. Her head was topped by a white cowboy hat.

The lady was walking two fluffy white dogs on leashes. As soon as they appeared outside the fence, one stood on its hind legs and began barking at Amanda in sharp, high-pitched yips. The dog strained so hard on its collar, it looked as if it would choke. The other dog yipped a little but never left the lady's side as she waddled up the driveway.

She seemed not to notice Amanda, but at the sidewalk turned left toward Turnberry, still swaying with each step. The one dog pulled toward Amanda, but the lady hauled steadily on its leash and dragged it along. The other dog still seemed not to know Amanda existed.

Amanda caught up to them, trying to think what to say to open a conversation. "Hello. Are those both your dogs?"

The elderly woman glanced around and smiled. "Yes, this is Tootsie, and the other one is Mitzi. Say hello to the young lady, girls."

Tootsie now struggled toward Turnberry, completely ignoring the girl skating slowly beside them. Mitzi kept her own sedate pace.

"I'm Amanda. I live in Cedar Terrace townhouses."

"How do you do?" the woman said affably. "I'm Rose Witcrest."

Hurray! thought Amanda. That was easy!

"I like your outfit," she continued.

"Do you? This is a square dancing costume, except for the boots, of course. I can't square dance any more, but I still like to wear the clothes and remember how much fun it was."

"Did you wear the hat square dancing?"

"Oh, no, that's to keep the sun out of my eyes. Of course, there's not any today, but there is a strong glare."

Amanda decided to go right to the subject. "Um, I was wondering . . .did Mary Jo Green go square dancing with you?"

Mrs. Witcrest looked surprised. "Oh, my. Did you know Mary Jo?"

Amanda took a deep breath. This was getting complicated. How could she tell Mrs. Witcrest that her friend Cindy had just met Mary Jo a few days earlier, even though Mary Jo had died a year ago?

"I didn't know her. I think my friend Cindy may have met her, but then–"

Mrs. Witcrest's face became wistful, almost sad. "Such a lovely lady. Mary Jo lived right there, you know." She indicated the house they were passing, a duplex with yellow siding. Number 3408 on the right was neat and trimmed. Number 3410 was overgrown with grass and weeds and had a "For Sale" sign in the front yard. "Mary Jo inherited the house on the right, number 3408, from her mother. A young family with two children lives there now."

"Who owns the other house?"

"A man who's never around very much. I'm glad he's selling that eyesore. Maybe the next owner will take better care of it."

Amanda said, "My friend and I went skating at the Roller Haven and saw Mary Jo Green's picture. We were just curious about her accident."

"Yes, that was terrible. Mary Jo did love roller skating. I went to see her perform in a show once."

Just then a voice started yelling from across the street. Amanda glanced up, startled. A boy of about ten years old, but big for his age and very fat, was standing on the sidewalk beside a huge oak tree. His hair was cut so short he looked almost bald.

"Hey, old lady!" he shouted. "Hey, midget! Why don't you take your two stupid dogs back to hell where they belong?"

Mrs. Witcrest merely smiled and waved. "Good evening, Billy. Tell your mother I said hello." She kept walking as though nothing had happened.

"Who in the world is that?" Amanda asked in amazement.

"Billy Bob Lawson. His mother's away at work all day and he stays home by himself. When he gets bored he comes out and insults people. I'm afraid he's going to do something bad one of these days."

"Little Black Sambo!" Now he was shouting at Amanda. "Get Aunt Jemima and go back to Africa where you belong!"

Amanda felt the heat rise in her face. She stopped and stared at him. Her heart started pounding so fast it was hard to catch her breath.

"Just ignore him," advised Rose. "That hurts him worse than insulting him back." When Amanda didn't move, Rose said insistently, "Come along. There's no point in getting upset."

Amanda realized the lady was right and began skating slowly again beside her. Billy Bob kept yelling but didn't try to follow. To drown out his voice,

Amanda asked, "How did Mary Jo's accident happen?"

"I have no idea."

"I thought you saw it."

"No, I was there at the time, but my back was turned." Mrs. Witcrest's face changed from sad to stern. "I wish I had seen it, so I could help the police catch and punish that hit-and-run driver."

Amanda's hips were beginning to hurt from skating so slowly. She wished she could stop and rest. "Could you tell me what happened?"

"We were walking our dogs in the evening, just about now. I didn't always feel like going out, but on days when I did, I waited for Mary Jo. Her dog Mitzi and my dog Tootsie were from the same litter, you know. That's how we met each other, when we went to a neighbor's house to pick up puppies that were being given away. I took Mitzi after Mary Jo died. Of course, someone had to go and get Mitzi from where she had run off into the woods.

"I only walk the dogs a couple of times a week now. They usually just run in the back yard, but they do need the discipline of a leash."

"Um, I was wondering—what was Mary Jo wearing that day?"

Mrs. Witcrest seemed surprised. "Why, I really don't remember. Is it important?"

"I guess not. I just—was curious." *Curious whether she was wearing a blue dress and high heels*, thought Amanda. *Because then I could be sure it was the same lady Jennifer and Cindy met.*

They were approaching the intersection with Turnberry. The white diagonal stripes of the crosswalk stood out clearly against the black street. Mrs. Witcrest slowed; Amanda was glad to halt and give her legs a rest.

Rose Witcrest dipped her head toward the middle of the street. "It was right out there. The sun was very bright, not like today with no sun. Mary Jo wanted to cross the street and walk along by the woods, but I decided to turn around and go home because I was tired.

"Mary Jo stepped into the crosswalk with Mitzi and I turned my back. I had only gone a few feet when I heard a loud screech of brakes. I looked back and saw Mary Jo lying in the street. Her blue skirt was all gathered up around her hips and one of her shoes was missing. Mitzi was running off into the woods across the road, and Tootsie started going crazy."

Amanda felt a thrill as Mrs. Witcrest described Mary Jo's clothing. The lady probably just didn't remember it before.

"I hurried to Mary Jo as quickly as I could—I can't run any more, you know. First I saw her blue high-heeled shoe lying in the gutter. Then I saw streaking off down the avenue a big, dark-colored car. I thought it must have been the one that struck her. It disappeared around that curve without stopping.

"Then a couple more cars came along. The drivers stopped and one of them called 9-1-1 on his cell phone. An ambulance came and took Mary Jo to the hospital. I was having a heck of a time keeping Tootsie calmed down. I don't think Mary Jo ever regained consciousness." Mrs. Witcrest shook her head. "It was very sad. Mary Jo was a good friend to me." The lady's eyes reddened and became glassy with tears.

Amanda felt her own eyes sting. She looked away, embarrassed.

But she had to ask something. "Why was she walking her dog in high heels?"

Mrs. Witcrest stared at her. "Why, what a strange question. I told you I didn't remember what she was wearing."

Then the lady turned her back on the intersection. "It's been very nice meeting you, Amanda. Here, Tootsie. Come on, Mitzi. Time to go home."

Amanda was suddenly feeling depressed. "Thank you for talking to me about Mary Jo."

"You're quite welcome. I hope we see each other again sometime." As she set off, one dog walked calmly just ahead of its owner. The other followed and then ran ahead, panting happily, its tongue lolling outside its wide-open mouth.

Amanda lowered herself to the grass for a rest. She leaned back on her hands and watched them walking away. Mrs. Witcrest shifted slowly from one leg to the other while Tootsie's long, pale fur trembled with her quick-trotting feet. Yet Amanda felt Mrs. Witcrest and that dog were very suited to each other. Whereas Mitzi . . . that was a dog for a real lady. Was that what Mary Jo Green had been?

Amanda was pushing herself upward when she heard a woman's voice.

"Hello, Amanda."

The girl jerked around so fast that she fell back onto the grass. Was it–? Could it be–?

It was.
Mary Jo Green stood smiling at her.
Amanda was meeting the ghost at last.

Chapter 9
Strange Ideas

Amanda couldn't speak. She stared at the woman with the reddish-blonde hair, the blue dress and high heels. She looked like a solid human, not a ghost at all. But her eyes were a light, supernatural green, even from ten or so feet away.

Finally Amanda forced a couple of breaths into her lungs and got the words out. "Are you—are you Mary Jo?"

The woman smiled. "How do you know my name?"

The next words came out in a rush. Amanda wasn't sure they made sense. "My friend Cindy. She told me. She met you last Saturday. And Barbara at the skating rink told me. I really like your picture. You're wearing a pink costume with jewels the same color as your eyes. Pink is my favorite color."

Mary Jo look wistful. "I miss Barbara so much. I wish I could see her. And I miss skating."

"Why—why don't you come to the rink?"

Mary Jo looked down. "Oh, that's all over for me now." She turned away and stared into the woods across the street.

Or maybe just into that intersection? Amanda wondered.

Amanda was able to stand now, but once upright she remained rooted in her spot, afraid to move any closer or speak. Suddenly Mary Jo turned back, eyes glowing like a neon sign. "Can you do something for me?"

"Me? Do what?" Amanda began to feel dizzy; it was hard to breathe again. She thought she was about to float away and couldn't stop it.

The ghost took a step closer. Amanda's control returned enough that she backed away the same distance.

"I want you to find a car for me." Suddenly Mary Jo's look became one of sadness combined with confusion. "I ought to know who it belongs to but I just can't remember."

Amanda could barely speak. "You wanted Cindy to go to the skating rink and Jennifer to find your dog. Now you want me to find the car."

Mary Jo smiled. "Oh, you found Mitzi. I saw her with you. Thank you."

"Rose found her, not me. Do you know who was driving it? The car, I mean."

Mary Jo seemed about to speak. Then a strange thing happened. She suddenly stared past Amanda and those green eyes became very round, as if seeing something they were afraid of.

Then Mary Jo was gone.

She didn't fade or drift away. Amanda was looking right at her. One second Mary Jo was standing there in front of Amanda. The next there was nothing but empty sidewalk and street. It was as if someone had shut off a light switch, and Mary Jo was the light that went out.

Amanda gaped. She looked behind herself. Was someone coming up the sidewalk? No, no one there. A couple of cars were passing in each direction, but none of them were dark blue.

She stared around, disoriented. What should she do now?

She decided it was time to hurry home and tell Cindy.

●●●

Jennifer Smallwood was tired of being stuck in the house. At the end of supper in the dining room, she announced to her mother, "I think I'd like to go out for a walk. In the orchard."

Mrs. Smallwood frowned over her dietetic dessert. She was wearing a pale blue summer dress that set off the elaborate hairdo fashioned high on her head. Victor had taken her to the beauty parlor in Fern Oak while Jennifer had been at ice skating practice. "This late at night? No, that's impossible."

"Mom, it's summer, remember? The sun won't set for another hour. Besides, I won't even leave our own yard. I just want to explore the orchard. I'm always inside a house or a car or a skating rink, never outdoors."

Mrs. Smallwood frowned. "Only if I come with you."

Jennifer frowned back. "I'm not a baby! I can go outside by myself."

"As you proved the other day when you snuck away from home. You and I will go out to the back yard together."

"Excuse me, Mrs. Smallwood," offered Mrs. Smith, who was clearing away the dishes. "Perhaps you should spray yourself with insect repellant first. Mosquitoes are very heavy this year."

Alarm showed on Lorraine Smallwood's face. "I hate insects!" She considered a moment. "Jennifer, you may not go farther than just inside the trees. I'll spray you before you go out."

Mrs. Smith brought a can of aerosol repellant. Jennifer submitted silently, gritting her teeth, while her mother covered every bare spot of skin except Jennifer's face. For that Mrs. Smallwood sprayed repellant onto her own hands and wiped it on her daughter's cheeks, chin, and forehead. Mrs. Smith waved a magazine to fan the fumes away so Jennifer could breathe.

Finally Mrs. Smallwood was done. She replaced the lid on the spray can. Jennifer gritted her teeth but made it look like a smile. "Thanks, Mom," she said, walking toward the back door. "See you in a little while."

"Maybe I should have Victor go with you."

"I'll stay in the yard like I promised!" Jennifer hurriedly closed the door and ran down the back steps.

She walked sedately across the back lawn to the peach trees, conscious of her mother's eyes on her from a kitchen window the whole way. Once inside the small orchard she lingered to select a piece of ripe fruit and take a bite. She stood and studied its yellow-orange interior. When she had finished eating the peach, she held its tan oval seed in her hand. The seed had a point on each end and bore strange, pitted coruscations over its surface.

She turned her head slightly to see back over her shoulder. Her mother had lost interest, as Jennifer had known she would, and was now turning away from the window. Soon she had disappeared into the room. Jennifer threw down the peach pit. She began walking normally until she couldn't see the window clearly any more. She increased her pace until she was running, almost out of the orchard and into the regular woods. She curved around to Smallwood Lane, and when she reached it, followed it toward Turnberry.

She'd obeyed her mother to the letter all day long: taken her ballet lesson, then her skating lesson; come home and eaten lunch, then gone back with her mother to Silver Spring to try on that blasted new costume again. It was not quite finished yet. They'd gotten home just in time for supper, and Jennifer had been close to screaming.

Now, at last, she could be by herself to check on something that had occurred to her. She kept following Smallwood, looking back often to be sure Victor wasn't coming after her in the Cadillac.

She remembered every fact about Mary Jo Green's death. She ran them all through her head as she approached that intersection. Once she'd reached it, she stood at the corner and stared out into the middle of the road. It was getting on toward twilight. Automobile headlights illuminated her face and passed on by. They came from each direction on Turnberry, and from in front and behind her along Smallwood Lane. Lost in her own unhappy thoughts, she hardly noticed them.

A dark blue car.

Jennifer was getting a very strange idea.

•••

"Oh, my gosh," gasped Cindy, "what did she say? What was she wearing? Did she talk to you? Oh, what did she say?"

"She said 'Hello, Amanda.' Then she said she wished she could go skating. And she was wearing high heels."

"I told you that. So did Jennifer."

"But she had been walking her dog. Who walks a dog in high heels?"

"Yeah, Mom always takes her high heels off as soon as she gets home from work. She says at the end of the day her feet hurt."

"Right. I'll bet Mary Jo would have changed into tennis shoes or sandals with flat soles."

"Maybe she was wearing something else when she died."

"Don't ghosts have to go on wearing the same things as when they're killed? That's the way it was in those movies, you know, *Beetlejuice* and *The Sixth Sense*."

"Well, maybe they can wear anything they want to. Tell me again how she disappeared."

Amanda described it again: how Mary Jo's eyes grew wide and frightened, how she just blinked out as if someone had flicked a switch. Then Amanda asked, "Are you over being sick? Because I think you should help me tomorrow. I want to go see those people who live in Mary Jo's old house."

"Yeah, that's a good idea, and I'm real tired of being inside."

Cindy heard muffled voices from Amanda's end of the phone.

"I have to go," said Amanda. "Dad needs the phone." She whispered, "I'm already in trouble because I was late for dinner."

"Okay. Talk to you tomorrow, and don't forget to call me first thing in the morning."

• • •

Cindy hung up the kitchen phone and closed the blinds on the darkening sky. Then she began to clear away her mother's supper dishes. Cindy had only been able to eat some clear chicken broth. She unloaded the dishwasher and put in the dirty stuff. There was room for more, but she'd run it tomorrow after it was full. That was a way of saving money on electricity that her mother had explained to her.

Cindy went upstairs to her mother's room and stood in the doorway. There was something she wanted to ask about. Two things, in fact.

Valerie Buford was sitting on her bed and using the night stand as a desk to write out checks for bills. The only other piece of furniture in the room was a bureau; the three were a used set she had bought at a thrift store like Cindy's bedroom furniture and the basement couch. There were no curtains on the windows in here either, only plastic venetian blinds.

"I'm done in the kitchen, Mom. You can go downstairs and use that table."

"I'm almost finished here." Her mother sighed and shook her head. "I swear, I love owning my own home, but paying a mortgage every month sure does take a lot of money."

Cindy frowned. "Oh, gosh, have we spent a lot this month?"

"Oh, no, we've been very frugal. But certain expenses just won't go away. I'm hoping there's enough for us to make it until the end of the month."

"But, Mom, that's another week and a half. Didn't Dad send you a check this month?"

Her mother almost snorted. "Yes, but a hundred dollars doesn't go very far when spread over thirty days. It's the same money he would be spending on food and other stuff for you if you were there with him instead of here with me. But he acts like it's a big hardship. Give me a break."

Cindy hung her head and turned away.

"Cindy, did you want something?"

"I just . . . would you have more money to spend if I weren't here?"

"Probably not." But Cindy saw the way her mother's head ducked, like it always did when she wasn't really telling everything.

"Well, I guess I'll take a bath and go to bed."

Cindy ran warm water into the basin and added some detergent. Then she put her bandannas in to soak. They were getting very frayed around the edges, and she wondered when she might be able to afford new ones.

She ran her bath water and shut it off while the level was still low so as not to run up the water bill. She bathed quickly and dried off, then rinsed the bandannas and hung them over the shower curtain rod.

She had wanted to ask her mother if there was any way she could take skating lessons from Barbara McAllister. And she wanted to ask about something else even more important.

But it didn't look as if either was going to be possible.

Chapter 10
Mysterious Visitors

On Friday morning, Jennifer did not feel like getting out of bed.

She had not slept well the night before. Her mother had been M-A-D when Jennifer got home after dark. Now Mrs. Smallwood stood in the bedroom doorway, her silk nightgown twisted sideways where her hand gripped her hip, her well-groomed face looking as if it were about to explode.

Mrs. Smith was sitting on Jennifer's bed, studying a thermometer. She shook her white curls. "You don't have a temperature." She stood and shucked the disposable plastic cover off the thermometer into the wastebasket.

"This is the second time this week you've missed skating practice," Mrs. Smallwood scolded icily.

"Mom, I don't feel good." Jennifer kept her face toward the wall and her eyes closed.

"There could be something going round," noted Mrs. Smith. "She wouldn't necessarily have a fever."

Mrs. Smallwood looked sharply at the housekeeper as if wondering whose side she was on. Then she turned away. "Well, perhaps she really is sick." She said back over her shoulder, "Get some sleep, Jennifer," and left the room.

Mrs. Smith followed and closed the door. But still as Jennifer lay still, her mind and body were all in turmoil. What was she going to do?

•••

Valerie Buford usually wore business-like skirts or pants, button-up shirts, and medium heels when she went to work. Today she had on white capris, a black tee shirt, and running shoes, although she carried her briefcase and purse when she came into Cindy's bedroom.

"I'm leaving for work now, Cindy. I'm glad you're feeling better."

Cindy opened her eyes sleepily, then widened them in surprise. Her voice croaked like a frog's. "Mom, you're not going to work like that?"

"Casual Friday, remember? The company just instituted it. We get to wear whatever we want to the office as long as it's not 'obnoxious or risque.'"

"What does 'risque' mean?"

"Never mind. Look, I'll be home an hour early this afternoon, about 4:30. We'll go out and get something to eat, all right? So don't be off somewhere else when I get home."

"Where will we go?"

"Maybe a pizza place or a hamburger joint. Nothing expensive, okay?"

"I don't want any more pizza!" Cindy groaned.

"Right, that's what made you sick. Well, try to think of something." Cindy's mom kissed her goodbye, then went downstairs and out of the house.

Cindy looked at the clock. It was early yet, only around eight a.m. She tried to go back to sleep but was too excited. Finally she went into her mother's room and called Amanda. "When can you come over?"

Amanda was eating breakfast. "I'll have to call you later. I still have to help my mom."

Cindy hung up and went back to bed. But the phone began ringing again; she ran across the hall and caught it on the fourth ring.

"Hello?"

"This is Jennifer." The girl was whispering.

Cindy was so surprised it was a few moments before she could respond. "What's wrong?"

"Nothing. I didn't go to practice today. My mother thinks I'm sick. Look, I got on the Internet and learned a bunch of stuff about Mary Jo Green and how she died."

"Amanda went out yesterday and found that lady who was a witness, Rose Witcrest. She's really old. She lives a couple of blocks from Mary Jo's house."

Jennifer recognized the name. "Amanda talked to her?"

"Yeah, for a long time, and learned a bunch of stuff."

There was a pause. "Can you come over today?" Jennifer asked.

"To your house?" Now Cindy was astonished.

"Yes."

Cindy did not want face Jennifer's unpleasant mother. She began looking for excuses not to visit. "Well–Amanda and I are going to go see the people living in Mary Jo's old house."

"I'd like to come along."

Cindy thought hard. She hadn't liked the way Jennifer had acted on Wednesday. "Aren't you supposed to be sick? Your mother probably won't let you leave the house or let anyone come over."

"Oh, right." Jennifer was quiet again. Then, "Can you call me back and tell me what you find out?"

"Okay. Give me your number. How did you find mine?"

"I looked on the internet for a Buford on Cedar Terrace."

Cindy wrote down Jennifer's number, said goodbye, and hurriedly hung up the phone. She had to decide whether she wanted this girl for a friend.

•••

Jennifer placed the receiver of her princess phone back in its cradle and climbed under the covers, feeling more miserable than she had for a long time.

She needed someone to talk to.

She drifted off to sleep again. A while later there were some unaccustomed noises from downstairs. Jennifer jerked upright in bed.

The banging continued. There was never *any* noise in this house! What was going on?

Then she realized it was coming from the front door.

•••

At ten a.m. the doorbell rang. Cindy answered it, her skates already laced on her feet. She wore a clean blue tank top; the newly washed bandannas were tied on her arms.

"Are you ready?" Amanda asked breathlessly. She had on pink tee shirt and shorts. "I can only be out an hour. I have to go back and babysit my brother while my mother goes to the beauty parlor."

"Let's go." Cindy shut the door and held onto the railing to clamber down the steps. The two girls sped off toward Smallwood Lane.

They raced to the duplex house where Mary Jo had lived -- 3408 on the right. At the sidewalk in front, they had to stop and catch their breaths. Amanda panted as she bent forward with her hands on her knees. Cindy sat on the concrete and leaned back, her chest rising and lowering like a winded dog's. Sweat was pouring down both of their faces. After about a minute, though, they were breathing almost normally.

"Come on," said Amanda, "let's knock on the door." She skated up the driveway with Cindy right behind her. A little curve of sidewalk led from the driveway to the porch on the right. At the porch they went up the steps, where Amanda found a doorbell and rang it.

They heard children's voices and realized the sounds were coming from behind the house.

"Let's go to the fence," said Amanda.

They stepped off the porch and walked on the lawn to the right side of the house, where there was a white fence that surrounded the back yard. The fence came to the bottoms of their necks, so they could see over it easily. The yard was filled with colorful toys, a plastic slide, and a kiddie pool.

A brown-haired woman and two light-haired children were splashing in the inflated pool. The woman looked up. "Hello. May I help you?"

"Hi. I'm Amanda Carter, and this is Cindy Buford. We live over on Cedar Terrace."

The lady rose from the water and took a towel from a nearby lounge chair. The two children jumped out and ran to the fence. Neither of them looked old enough for kindergarten. Their mother followed them.

"Nice to meet you. I'm Mrs. Grant, and these are Karen and Brandon."

"Hello," answered the two girls.

"I can do cartwheels," said Karen. She bent over and placed her small hands on the grass, pushed one foot into the air, then hopped onto it as she lifted the other foot high.

Brandon asked, "Are you selling cookies?" He was very chubby.

"No."

Mrs. Grant ruffled his hair and laughed. "What can we do for you?"

Amanda began, "We were wondering if this was the house where Mary Jo Green used to live."

"And we wondered if you knew her," added Cindy.

Mrs. Grant's face went from friendly to worried. She hesitated before she answered them. "Oh, this is the house, but we never met the lady. We bought this place about six months ago. It was terrible how she died, wasn't it?"

"Do you know the story about it?"

She seemed friendly again. "Goodness, everybody around here knows it. The neighbors tell it to their kids to keep them from crossing Turnberry, and we do too, of course."

"But what happened?" asked Cindy.

Amanda poked her. "I already told you."

Cindy frowned. "Well, I want to hear it for myself."

Mrs. Grant looked from one girl to the other. Then she said, "Well, it was really awful. The lady was walking her dog and she tried to cross Turnberry when a car hit her. Everybody figures the sun was in the driver's eyes. Anyway, it was a hit-and-run. The car drove off without stopping and nobody ever found out who it was."

"That's pretty much what the newspapers said," agreed Cindy.

"See?" demanded Amanda.

"But why are you girls so interested in the story? You didn't know her, did you."

"Oh, no. I just moved into the neighborhood a month ago, and Amanda—"

"My family's only been here a little longer. We bought our townhouse in May."

"Well, I'm surprised your own neighbors haven't told you all about it." Mrs. Grant stood a moment as if unable to decide what to do next. Then she looked at her two children, who were chasing each other around the yard. "Well, kids, I think it's time to go in for lunch."

Amanda glanced at her watch. It was only ten-thirty in the morning.

"Okay!" shouted Brandon, and ran for the back steps.

"I want to keep playing," pouted Karen.

"It was nice talking to you." Mrs. Grant took her daughter's hand. "Come again sometime."

Brandon opened the door and went inside. Mrs. Grant climbed the steps.

"Wait!" said Cindy. "Does anybody know why she was wearing high heels to walk her dog?"

Mrs. Grant paused. "I've never heard that. How in the world did you know?"

"We saw—"

"Rose Witcrest told me," interrupted Amanda. "She was Mary Jo's friend."

"Would the people next door know anything?" asked Cindy.

"Oh, that side has been empty since we moved in." Mrs. Grant shooed her daughter through the door and closed it behind them.

The girls stared at the closed door a moment, then pulled their heads back from where they'd been jutted over the fence.

Said Amanda, "It's kind of early for lunch."

"Sure is."

"I don't think she wanted to talk to us."

"I guess we should go," said Cindy.

"Yeah."

They walked carefully across the grass to the driveway and stopped to study the house they had just visited.

Cindy looked at 3410, the left side of the duplex. She looked at the "For Sale" sign that sat in the very front of the yard next to the sidewalk. "I wonder why nobody lives there."

Amanda indicated the sign. "Rose said it's been up for sale a long time."

"It looks like it. The yard must be four feet tall and full of weeds." Then Cindy gasped. "Someone's inside! The curtain just moved!"

"Oh, come on," Amanda objected. "There's no one in there."

"I saw the curtain move," insisted Cindy. The closed white curtains in the front picture window had given a sudden twitch at the center, as if someone had parted them just enough to look out.

"Probably the real estate agent."

"But there's no car in the driveway."

"Look, I have to get home. We can do some more tomorrow." Amanda started for the sidewalk.

Cindy followed, but slowly. "I'm going to stay and keep watch."

"How?"

"Hide behind that tree." She indicated the huge gnarled oak a little way down on the other side of the street.

"Talk to you later." Amanda raced off. Cindy crossed the street and skated to the tree. She took a seat on a thick, raised root that was on the far side from 3410 so that she was partially hidden from view of the duplex. She was determined to wait out the person inside that house.

She didn't have long.

•••

The white garage door began rising from the concrete driveway. Cindy stood and pressed up hard against the tree to hide behind its bulk. She extended her face just past the rough bark to watch what was going on. Sure enough, that garage door was slowly opening.

"Hey, you! What are you doing in my front yard!"

Cindy jerked around, startled. A heavy boy stood on the sidewalk glaring at her. His hair was very short, cut in a burr. He didn't even look as old as Cindy, but he was lots bigger.

"Go away!" he shouted. "You don't belong here!"

"You don't own the sidewalk. Anyone can sit here." She sneaked another look around the tree. The garage door was past halfway up and still moving.

"You're loitering and you're stalking somebody." The boy's voice was very close. She could feel his hot breath on the back of her head. It smelled bad. "Get lost or I'll call the police!" he concluded.

The garage door was open. Cindy stood. Her legs had grown stiff; she bounced a little to loosen them up. A red car appeared, backing out the driveway. Cindy thought a man was driving.

"Did you hear me? Get lost!" A hand grabbed her right shoulder and yanked her around.

Angry now, Cindy poked two fingers into the boy's eyes. He gasped and clenched at his face with both hands. She raised a knee into the soft spot at the bottom of his belly.

"Ow!" He fell to his knees, howling.

"Don't mess with a street kid from Baltimore!" she shouted, and started down the sidewalk in pursuit of the escaping car. Because of that kid, she hadn't gotten a good look at the driver.

The red car had a good head start, but had to screech to a halt at the corner because cars were passing on the busy street. Cindy bent forward almost double, pushing so hard her feet were moving almost straight out to the sides.

The car was making a right turn. Cindy was close enough to make out the Maryland license plate: HAK 501. Then the car gained the street and sped away. As she reached the corner, the red car was disappearing around the blind curve.

She stared after it, then looked across the intersection, down the tree-lined road that was the continuation of Smallwood Lane. Should she skate down there and tell Jennifer?

But what was a more important question, how could she trace a car's owner through its license plate number?

Chapter 11
Wishes Partially Fulfilled

Jennifer was suddenly happy because she had an idea what the noises downstairs might be.

She left her bedroom. She heard her father's voice coming from behind the closed door of the study at the foot of the stairs. Her face formed a deep smile of pleasure. She hurriedly descended and ran across the wide hallway to wait outside until he had finished his phone call.

When she heard him say, "I'll talk to you tomorrow, Mr. Coronado," she tapped lightly on the dark oak door, then opened it and stepped inside the huge room.

"Daddy!"

"Angel!" Roger Smallwood opened his arms. "You're finally awake!"

When she was younger she would have run to her father, and she almost did that now. But suddenly she remembered to walk sedately and keep her poise, as her mother had been recently lecturing her. That gave Mr. Smallwood time to stand and watch her approach. His face was beaming, and Jennifer felt her expression match his.

Warmth filled Jennifer's chest as she embraced her father. Suddenly she found herself sobbing.

"What's wrong?" He was alarmed.

"Oh, Daddy, I've missed you so much. It's so lonely here."

"Why, you have your mother and your friends at the rink." Jennifer hung her head. "Oh, I know—you miss the people from school now that it's summer. Why don't you invite them over?"

Then came Mrs. Smallwood's voice. She must have silently entered the room. "Some of her friends did come over for a few minutes. New ones, from around here. I—was quite surprised."

Jennifer looked around at her mother's haughty face. The woman continued, "Jennifer went *roller skating* with them."

"Well, that sounds like fun," commented Mr. Smallwood.

"She skipped ice skating to go." Lorraine Smallwood frowned icily at her daughter.

"How many times did she skip?"

"Just the once, Daddy. It was two days ago."

"For Pete's sake, Lorraine. The girl needs to have fun sometime. She's had an ice skating lesson every day for the past year except Christmas and Easter."

"And *that* was only because Jacques wanted the day off," commented Mrs. Smallwood. "I was not happy." After a pause she continued, "But she missed today too! She said she was sick."

"Are you sick?"

Jennifer looked down again. "I don't feel all that well."

He looked at his wife. "Lorraine," he began, in a voice that was a combination of warning and frustration.

"And she left the house the other day without telling anyone! Then yesterday she went out and came back after dark!"

Jennifer felt her cheeks growing hot. "I went for a walk," she mumbled.

Now her father was directing a stern look at her.

"Dad, I'm not a baby! I should be able to leave the house now and then. I have to stay inside here or at the ice rink or the dance studio like everywhere I go is some kind of prison."

Her father sighed. "Well, I know what that's like." He looked suddenly weary. It was an expression Jennifer had noticed lately when he talked about his job. He continued, "But you can't stay out after dark!"

Mrs. Smallwood spoke again. "Roger, she'll never be a champion if she doesn't practice."

"Even Peggy Fleming had a day off," he reminded his wife.

Ice skaters all knew the story of how much Peggy Fleming, competing in the 1968 Olympics, wanted to skip her lesson to attend the party for the whole USA Olympic team. Her coach had refused to let her go. For once defiant, Peggy had threatened not to compete if she had to stay away. Finally her coach backed down, and Peggy went to the party with the other athletes from the U.S. The next day she won the Gold Medal in Ladies' Figure Skating.

Jennifer felt nervous about her father bringing up the subject. Mrs. Smallwood had always been on the side of the coach and let everyone know it.

Now her mother turned away. "Luncheon is ready," she said over her shoulder, and left the room.

Jennifer relaxed a little.

"How long will you be home, Daddy?" Jennifer felt cheerful over her father's support.

"A while, I hope. Mr. Langford is training a new man to make overseas sales trips and give me a break. I'm getting too old for it."

Her father did look older. There were dark circles under his eyes, and his skin was paper thin, stretched tight but wrinkled. He had lost weight, too; where his stomach had once formed a little pouch, now it was flat, and his pants seemed to hang loosely on his hips.

Such a difference between her parents. Her father was only a year older than her mother, though he looked much older. Still, he didn't take time to be driven to beauty spas and hairdressers every couple of weeks. He didn't spend hours at home giving himself facials, or just relaxing around the house.

Jennifer often wondered why her father worked so hard. He didn't need to, according to her mother. She said they had plenty of money. But, her mother said, he had inherited a hard work ethic from his father, to whom it was passed down from his father and grandfather, all the way back to the original founders of the Smallwood Plantation. They did not believe in laziness.

On the other hand, they believed in enjoying life as well. Jennifer hoped her father was going to take some time now to relax and have fun.

"So you'll be working around here for a while?"

"It looks like it, Honey!"

She took his arm. "Let's go in to lunch."

•••

Cindy called Amanda. "There was a person in that house and a car came out of the garage and I followed it and got the license number! A man was driving."

"Wow! Was it the car that killed Mary Jo?"

"No, it was red. Can you come over?"

"My mom's not back yet."

"Jennifer called me this morning."

"You didn't tell me!"

"I forgot. I don't think I like her."

"Me either."

One of those pauses occurred while each girl thought. Then Cindy said, "I'm going to the library to find out how to trace a license plate."

"You just said it's not the car."

"Well, why was that man hiding from us? He must've heard us talking to Mrs. Grant and he has to have something to do with it. I know! I'll bet I can find out who owns that house, too!"

Cindy heard a wail from the other end of the phone.

"I've got to go. Tayvon's hurt himself. Call me and tell me what you find out. Maybe I'll try to do something on Dad's computer."

They hung up. Cindy left her skates home when she went out.

•••

At the library she asked how to learn the names of the owners of a house.

"Why in the world would you want to know that!" the librarian asked. "Surely *you're* not planning to buy a house."

"I'm, uh, helping my mother."

The lady looked unconvinced, but said, "Well, it is public information. You have to get it from the county land records office, and I'm not sure if it's on-line."

"So it would be under Guilford County, Maryland?"

"If it exists on-line, yes."

Cindy logged on and did a search. The information *was* in the Guilford County database. She printed out several sheets of paper.

Then she tried to log onto the Department of Motor Vehicles website and find the owner of Maryland license plate HAK 501. But the information was restricted.

She'd had enough for one day. She ran home to call Amanda.

"That side of the duplex has been owned by a guy named Jonathan Leifer for ten years. He has another place over in Baltimore County that he bought not too long ago. I'll bet that was him in the red car. And some people named Grant *do* own 3408, the other side of the duplex."

Amanda said, "I'll go on-line and see if I can find out anything. I'll come over when my mom gets home. There can't be anything else she needs me to do for this party tonight."

●●●

Cindy sat with her hand on the telephone. She had told Jennifer she would call back and keep her informed. She didn't really want to, but . . .

Cindy dialed Jennifer's number. An elderly lady's voice answered. It did not sound like Jennifer's mother.

"May I speak to Jennifer?"

"Who's calling, please?"

"Cindy Buford."

"Just a moment, please."

Cindy had to wait about five minutes. Jennifer sounded breathless when she answered. "I've got it, Mrs. Smith." There was a click on the line, then Jennifer's voice again. "I'm sorry I took so long. I had to run upstairs to my room so nobody could hear. What did you find out?"

Cindy recited a synopsis of all the things she and Amanda had done that day. "Now if I could just find a way to learn about that license number."

"What was the number again?"

"HAK 501. It's a Maryland license plate."

"Maybe my dad can help. His company deals with DMV all the time. They have a bunch of transport trucks that carry machinery all over the United States and they import machinery from all over the world."

"DMV?"

"Department of Motor Vehicles."

"Isn't your dad out of town?"

"Oh, he just got back today!" Jennifer did not have to say that she was happy her father was home; Cindy could hear it in her voice.

"That's great! How long has he been gone?"

"Over three months. He's really been working hard. He says he's going to take it easy now, spend more time at home."

"I bet you're glad."

"Yes! Anyway, look, I have to go. We're going out to eat in a little while and I have to get ready."

"Okay. Well, don't forget to ask your dad."

"I won't. I'll call when I know something."

They hung up. Cindy wondered if Jennifer would actually be able to get any information on the red car and its license plate.

•••

Amanda said, "Mom, could I go over to Cindy's for a while?"

"What? No, I need you to help me make finger foods for the serving platters." Decorative paper platters, the heavy-duty kind, were lined up on the kitchen table and counters. Mrs. Carter, her hair newly trimmed and set in a very stylish, short hairdo, was taking prepared vegetables, crackers, and dips from packages and putting them onto one tray. "You can take the sausages and cheeses from this bag and put them onto the two trays over on the table."

Amanda began opening plastic packages and arranging food on trays. "Mom, this food will spoil! The party's not until seven."

"I've made room in the fridge."

"After this can I go out?"

"You can't go anywhere. You have to babysit Tayvon."

"That's later! I'll only be gone an hour!"

"No." Her mother emphatically shook her head. "I have to get our own supper ready, and then I have to get dressed. I need you here."

Amanda felt like crying. She'd already been stuck in the house all day with Tayvon. Well, except for that trip in the morning to the Grants' house. But an hour looking after her little brother was like a week in prison.

Amanda tried one more thing. "Well, may I go on-line? I need to research something."

"What, ghosts and car wrecks? I don't think so."

"But—" Just then Amanda looked out the window and saw her father's car pulling into the parking space. "Why's Dad home early?"

"To get ready for the party. Come on, stack those plates in the fridge. I'll heat the lasagna in the microwave."

Amanda opened the refrigerator and saw more food in packages to be put onto trays later.

Her father came in the front door and into the kitchen. "How's my girl!" he exclaimed, and opened his arms for a hug from Amanda. When he was done squeezing her she asked, "Daddy, may I go on-line?"

He shook his head. "Maybe later. It's suppertime now."

He stepped over to his wife. "Hello, Darling." She turned around and they kissed each other briefly.

"Everything ready?" he asked.

"Just about. We'll put out all the food after the guests begin to arrive, and you can take care of the drinks."

"You only bought sodas, juices, and punch, right? No beer or other alcohol?"

"None."

Mrs. Carter put the hot lasagna on the table and sent Amanda to get Tayvon. Amanda went upstairs for her brother and found him in her parents' bedroom. He was playing with her mother's makeup.

He was in front of the dresser mirror. He had a small bottle in one hand and he was applying foundation to his face with the other. He grinned when he saw Amanda's aghast expression.

"Look at me! I'm a clown!"

Amanda saw the red marks around his mouth and the tubes of open lipstick on the dresser.

She shrieked and sank to the floor, then crawled under the bed. She knew she was going to get blamed for this one.

After she had lain face down under her parents' bed a couple of minutes, breathing carpet fibers and dust into her lungs, her father yelled up the stairs for her and Tayvon to come down to dinner. Amanda crawled back out. Now Tayvon was painting red lipstick around his eyes.

Amanda resigned herself to her fate. She took him into the bathroom and cleaned the makeup off him. She went back to her parent's bedroom and wiped off the dresser and the bedroom carpet. Then she led Tayvon downstairs for their meal. While she ate, she tried to figure how she could secretly go on-line and find some way to put him up for adoption.

•••

Victor drover Jennifer and her parents to an expensive restaurant, then waited outside, the way chauffeurs do.

The girl was quiet during dinner. She was thinking deeply about what she wanted to tell her father, wondering how and when she could bring up the subject of the dark blue car and the hit-and-run accident.

But looking at her parents together again in the glow of the table's candle, feeling a warm glow herself because her father was home, she began to wonder if it was really important.

By the time the meal was over and Jennifer had eaten her last bite of cherry truffle, the accident and the lady who had spoken to her no longer seemed important or even real.

That night, lying in bed, she was so happy that even the events of the previous week seemed far away. Her father was home! Things would be different now.

•••

Cindy and her mother went to a hamburger place for supper. While she ate a bowl of chili, Cindy worked up the courage to ask her mother a big, expensive favor.

"Mom?" asked Cindy.

"Mm,hmm?" Valerie was chewing her hamburger.

"I really like skating."

"Of course. You do it all the time."

"No, I mean, I like skating in a roller rink."

"Really? I thought you didn't like being stuck going round and round all the time."

"Well, it's not so bad when you can do free style. I mean, free stylers go really fast in every direction all over the floor. And they get to pick out the music they skate to."

"Kind of like you do when you go out to skate."

"Yes, but they don't wear Walkmans. They hear the music over the sound system. And they do great stuff, just like ice skaters on TV."

"So what are you telling me?"

"Well . . ." Cindy paused. Money was always such a problem. "I'd like to take skating lessons so I can do what the free style skaters do. I can already do some of that stuff, but I want to learn more."

"Skating lessons?"

"Yes. At Roller Haven Skating Rink. From Barbara McAllister."

"How much will that cost?"

"I've got a schedule here. It gives the amounts. I got it off the internet at the library today." Cindy pulled the printout from her pocket, unfolded it, and handed it across the table to her mother.

Valerie smiled. "Looks like we're getting our money's worth from that library card."

But Cindy frowned. "Library cards are free, I didn't pay anything for it!"

"I'm only joking." She read the schedule. "Beginner classes on Saturday afternoons at twelve o'clock and on Tuesday nights at six-thirty. Intermediate classes Sunday afternoons at twelve. Advanced classes Wednesday nights at six-thirty. The series of lessons lasts six weeks." Mrs. Buford looked up. "Skating classes aren't held in the summer. They start again in September."

"Right. We can save up money until then."

Mrs. Buford sighed. "Cindy, you're going back to your father when school starts."

Cindy looked down into her empty bowl, then up at her mother. "I don't want to go back there. I want to stay here."

Valerie Buford nodded. "I know you do. I want you to stay. But Cindy—a couple of months in the summer, with no heating bills and no warm clothes to buy—that's one thing. Staying here in winter costs a lot more. A hundred dollars a month from your father won't be enough. Besides which, he might not agree to let you stay, and then we'll be back to another court hearing and paying more lawyer bills."

Cindy felt like crying. "He doesn't want me there. It's only so he won't have to give you money. He doesn't have time for me, just for Peter and Linda. And I hate downtown Baltimore! It's a yucky place to live." She sniffed. "I wish I'd never had to leave where we lived in Cherry Hill before the divorce."

"So do I." Now Valerie Buford looked as if she were close to tears. She shook her head. "Look, I can't promise about the skating lessons. But I think we both should talk to your father about your coming here to stay. Maybe we can find a way."

Cindy smiled with reddened eyes. "Thanks, Mom. Um—could you take me and Amanda skating tomorrow?"

Chapter 12
Busy Saturday

Jennifer awoke Saturday morning feeling happier than she had in months. She hurried to get ready for her figure skating lesson and practice; her father was driving her today.

At The Ice House, Jacques smiled and skated over to shake Mr. Smallwood's hand. Jennifer stood holding her father's other arm. "Hello, Mr. Smallwood, how are you!" greeted Jacques' strong French accent.

"Doing fine, Jacques. Wanted to watch my little girl skate."

"She is doing very well, although she missed a couple of days this week." Jacques looked inquiringly at Jennifer. "You are not feeling well yesterday?"

"No, and on Wednesday I went roller skating instead." Jennifer said it rather primly, as if she'd been performing charity service.

"So I have heard. I hope you are not planning to switch to a new sport."

She grinned and answered impishly, "Not right now, but maybe later."

Jacques suppressed a laugh. "Yes, well, go and put on your skates. I will meet you on the ice. Good to see you, Mr. Smallwood." Jacques turned and glided to the middle of the ice, where he practiced graceful turns and arm positions.

Soon Jennifer joined him, and the lesson began.

When lesson and practice were over and they left the ice rink, they stopped at a diner for lunch. Driving home afterward, they were laughing and joking.

But as they entered Murrayville, and the closer they got to Smallwood Lane, the quieter Jennifer grew.

"Jennifer, what's wrong? You don't look good."

"Dad—I need to talk to you about something."

"Sure. What is it?"

"When we get home, before we go into the house—can we talk then?"

"Fine by me."

Soon they were passing by the peach orchards that bordered their driveway and Roger Smallwood had followed the driveway away from the circle in front of the house to park the limousine in the garage. Jennifer left the air-conditioned car for the outdoor humidity and walked slowly over to her mother's dark blue Mercedes.

She circled the car, studying the polished sheen that Victor had kept on it during its near-year of disuse. "Dad . . ."

Her father finished locking the Cadillac and came to stand beside her. "What is it, Honey? You don't look very happy."

She looked out through the garage doors—ancient but refurbished barn doors that had been on this land for generations—toward the centuries-old house just visible through the grove's maple trees. There, she knew, her mother was waiting for them.

"Dad, do you know that Mom hasn't driven this car in a long time? And she never goes anywhere any more."

Her father studied a garage wall. Its outside planks were centuries old, its insides reinforced and insulated so it looked like a modern garage within. Against the wall were metal storage shelves that contained motor oil, windshield wiper fluid, car polish, replacement headlights and interior bulbs, a tool box, everything Victor used to keep the automobiles in perfect condition. There was nothing at all interesting there.

Jennifer realized he didn't even see what he was looking at. His face was very sad and distracted, as if he were thinking about something a long way off.

He turned those sad eyes on her. "I know," he answered, nodding.

He knew?

Wait, he couldn't—

She reached inside her pocket, grabbed the folded papers. She'd get him to read them and tell her if they were true or not.

He continued, "But it's something I can't talk about or deal with right now."

"No? Well, we have to—I mean, it's so important, and . . ."

Jennifer stopped talking. There was so much desolation in her father's expression that her mouth just went silent and couldn't say anything else.

"Yes, Jennifer, it is important, and we will have to do something about it sometime. But not today."

He took her arm. They closed the garage doors and walked together through the sultry heat, up to the house where each of them had lived since their births.

•••

At 12:30 Cindy heard a knock at her front door. She was so excited she could feel thrills running through her stomach as she ran to answer it. There stood Amanda, skates slung over her shoulder. She was wearing denim shorts and a white tee shirt with pink valentine hearts all over it.

"Am I late?"

"You're early." Cindy spoke breathlessly around a bite of baloney sandwich. "We were just eating lunch. Come inside." Cindy had on a navy blue tank top that was getting too tight, and denim shorts; the clean bandannas were around her arms.

They went to the kitchen and sat at the table with Cindy's mom. Mrs. Buford asked, "How was your parents' party, Amanda?"

Amanda made a victimized face. "It was a party for them, but I was in a lunatic asylum!" She related her little brother's adventure with the makeup and her own efforts to clean it up. "Then I had to watch him the rest of the night. I didn't think Tayvon would ever go to sleep. When he did I was too tired to watch TV or anything and I just went to bed. I'm gonna take him out in the woods and leave him there."

"I'll bring Peter along," offered Cindy. Then she felt bad. Peter was just a little baby, not yet a year old. If she were lucky she'd never have to live with him again, just see him on visits.

She glanced at her mother, who was very carefully keeping no expression on her face.

Cindy gulped her sandwich and drink, and her mother finished eating, while Amanda sat with them at the kitchen table, drinking a glass of juice.

"Mrs. Buford, you're really going to talk to Barbara McAllister about private lessons?"

"I already did, on the phone. She said she could give you both a semi-private lesson today at 4:00. I told your mother that, and she agreed to pay for half the cost. Didn't she tell you?"

"She told me. I just wanted to make sure it was really true. Here, I brought the money." Amanda reached into her shorts pocket and counted out some paper bills to Mrs. Buford, then put back the remainder of the wad. "I need the rest for admission and a snack."

"Not pizza!" stated Cindy.

"It didn't make me sick."

"Well, it sure did me."

Cindy's mom rose. "Let's get going. I have errands to finish during the session. Then I can watch your lesson."

Cindy frowned as she put her plate next to the sink. "Why do you need to watch?" she grumbled. "What do you think she's going to teach us, how to destroy a wall with our skates?"

"No smart mouth, young lady. I know you never want me around any more, but if I'm paying for it, I have a right to see it. Now let's go."

They followed the familiar route to the Roller Haven. Cindy's mom let the girls out in front. "I'll be back at four o'clock. Don't skate so hard you wear yourselves out for the lesson."

Cindy rolled her eyes but said nothing.

There weren't as many birthday parties as the week before, so the floor had more space for skating without running over bad skaters and little kids every two feet. They did all the games and races, and Cindy and Amanda won, of course, but Cindy kept wondering where Barbara was. What if she didn't show up? What if they couldn't get a lesson? Cindy felt shivery and apprehensive. Barbara came in when the club skaters began to arrive, just before the session was over. Cindy's relief was so great she almost fell on the floor. "She's here!" she shouted.

"Don't yell so loud," Amanda said, frowning. "I'm right next to you."

Cindy rushed to the railing, Amanda behind her. They almost knocked over some people when they cut in front of them.

"Watch it!" snarled a girl a few years younger who could barely stand up.

"Nyah-nyah," Cindy mocked her.

"Sorry," answered Amanda.

"Barbara!" Cindy called, but Barbara was walking very fast and disappeared into the rink office.

Britt and Tiff came in the door wearing light blue skating outfits. Their mother, Carol Parton, and Garrett, the African-American figure skater, appeared right behind them. Donnie and Melanie, the young pairs skaters, came in next. All of them sat down and began putting on their skates.

Cindy skated over. "Hi," she said to Carol. "We're taking a lesson from Barbara today."

"Oh, good." She smiled. "We can use more skaters."

"More skaters!" shouted Garrett, smiling widely. "Yes! Welcome, girls! Join our club!"

Carol laughed. "He's always like that," she explained.

Barbara appeared, pushing the wide dustmop onto the floor. Cindy and Amanda skated over to her.

"Are you girls here for your lesson?"

"Yeah!" they chorused.

"Let me get the floor cleaned up and we can start."

"We'll sweep the floor," offered Cindy.

"Great. I can get some other stuff done."

Barbara gave them the mop and went to give instructions to the rink staff, who were cleaning up from the session and the birthday parties. Cindy and Amanda took the dustmop out to the floor and pushed it round the outside edge of the rink. It was harder than it looked, especially with two of them gripping the handle and trying not to trip each other. They shook the dirt out at the end of the floor just as they'd seen Barbara do, and started round again a little closer to the center. About the third time around they were getting tired, but they had reached the black line that separated the center area from the rest of the floor and club skaters were coming out to practice. By the time they had finished the center, Garrett, Brittany and Tiffany were doing figures, and Cindy was exhausted.

She and Amanda shook out the dirt one last time. Cindy leaned on the handle to hold herself up. "I'm too tired now to take a lesson."

"Don't tell your mom that. She's just coming in the door."

Cindy's mother was indeed walking to the railing near the front door. Cindy straightened up and waved. "Hi, Mom!" she said brightly.

Barbara reappeared. "Ready, girls?"

"Yes, we are," Cindy answered, a wide smile stretched across her teeth.

Barbara took them out to the floor. "Remember that people taking a lesson have the right of way, so right now others have to move out of your way, but during somebody else's lesson, you have to move." The two girls nodded. "All right, we're going to go through the basics. First, skate forward in what we call 'coke bottles.'" Barbara demonstrated. "While rolling down the floor you bend your knees deeply, push your skates to the side, straighten your knees some and pull your feet inward. If you had markers on the bottoms of your skates you would make wavy lines on the floor that go out and in like the shapes of old-fashioned Coca-Cola bottles. This movement gives you power and helps you roll faster."

The two girls tried it, going faster and faster down the floor until they were almost racing. They circled the floor once and braked to a stop next to Barbara.

"This is baby stuff," Cindy said. "I already know how to skate fast."

"It's a basic move," Barbara answered. "You need to learn it before doing more advance moves. Now turn around and do it backward."

"But—"

"Hush up and do it!" Amanda hissed in a sharp whisper.

The two girls turned backward and began forcing their feet out the same way, but it was not as easy. They had to bend at the waist and hold their chests over their bent knees in order to roll the opposite direction. They circled the rink again, this time not as quickly, but again Amanda was in the lead.

"I'm sure you've done both these moves when you've skated outside," Barbara remarked.

"Some," answered Amanda, "but we have to worry about cracks in the sidewalk when we're going backward."

The lesson went on. Barbara showed them how to "stroke" down the floor, which meant pushing hard onto one foot, yet looking graceful doing it, holding the other foot in the air behind them with their toes pointed. She taught them crosses, where they had to lift one foot, cross it over the other at the ankles, and place it on the floor right next to the other foot; they did crosses in front and behind, forward and backward. The girls each tripped and fell a couple of times.

The last thing they learned was how to stroke backward, which was a lot harder than stroking forward. Cindy again fell down several times as she tried to push backward with one foot, hold it in the air while rolling backward down the floor, then change to the opposite foot.

After a long time Barbara said the lesson was over. Cindy looked at the clock. The lesson had only lasted twenty minutes.

Barbara skated over to Cindy's mom. Cindy and Amanda followed. "Mrs. Buford?"

"Yes, I'm Cindy's mother. I guess you're Barbara. The girls never stop talking about you."

"Mom!" said Cindy, embarrassed.

Barbara laughed. "Well, they both have skating ability. Cindy especially could do Creative Solo, which is like expressive dancing but on skates. And Amanda has a lot of speed."

Cindy's mom took some money from her purse and handed it to Barbara. "Is that the right amount?"

"That's fine. Let me get you a receipt."

Barbara left for the office. Mrs. Buford said, "So how was the first lesson? Do you want to keep taking them?"

"Well, I didn't learn much," commented Cindy, "but I want to take more so I can be in a contest like these club skaters."

"How about you, Amanda?"

"Yeah, I like it. I'm going to ask my mom to let me keep coming."

Cindy asked her mother, "Can you afford lessons every week?"

"Maybe, if both of you keep taking together and Amanda pays for half. If you take them by yourself, I'm not sure."

"Well, I'm going to try to keep coming," Amanda said.

Barbara reappeared with a receipt for Cindy's mother. Cindy asked, "When are the skaters leaving for the championships?"

"Some have already gone. These people are flying out to Lincoln, Nebraska on Sunday." Barbara thought a moment. "I guess that's tomorrow. I'm so busy these days I can't keep track of anything. I'm flying out tomorrow myself. A few people aren't going until later in the week, just before their events."

Mrs. Buford put the receipt into her purse. Cindy thought of an important question. Without considering how Barbara might react, Cindy asked, "What day was Mary Jo Green going out last year?"

Barbara practically glared. "Why are you so interested in that subject?"

Cindy suddenly felt ashamed. "I—I just . . ."

"I really don't like talking about it." Barbara skated onto the floor and began giving a figure lesson to Tiff.

Cindy's mom raised her eyebrows at her daughter. Carol, who was leaning nearby on the railing, turned toward them and spoke. "Actually, a lot of us wonder what happened to Mary Jo. Did you know her?"

"No," answered Mrs. Buford.

"But we met—" began Cindy.

Amanda interrupted. "She lived in our neighborhood and we heard about her accident."

Carol nodded. "Yes, that was terrible. She finished fourth in the nation in Esquire Ladies' Figures the year before. She just missed getting third place. It was the closest she'd ever come to a national medal. Everybody expected she'd get a medal at the championships last year. But she was killed right before she was supposed to fly out to Lincoln, and they never caught the person whose car hit her. Next Monday will be the anniversary of her death."

"Actually the anniversary is Tuesday the 26th," corrected Cindy.

Carol's expression was glum.

"Well, it happened on a Monday, and I'll always think of it as Black Monday."

"Could it have been somebody who was jealous of her skating?" asked Amanda.

Carol laughed out loud. "Jealous of Mary Jo? She helped keep this club going! She was always bringing kids in and getting them to start skating. In fact, she's the reason I started to bring Tiff and Britt here."

"Really?" asked Cindy.

"No kidding?" said Amanda.

"That's right. We were in her travel agency one day trying to get tickets to go to Florida. She started talking about skating and how cute the girls would look out on the floor in fancy costumes. We came for a session and watched practice, and next thing I knew my girls were taking lessons. We've been coming here more than two years now."

"That's pretty much what happened with us," Cindy said. "One day I was out sidewalk skating and Mary Jo—"

"Do your girls only skate figures?" asked Amanda, punching Cindy with her elbow as she spoke.

"No, they do free style too." Carol looked curiously at Cindy. "What were you just saying?"

"Umm—nothing." Cindy looked down at the carpet and wondered what Barbara would use to scrape up all the pieces of gum embedded there.

"We really need to go, Cindy," said Mrs. Buford. "I have to start supper."

Cindy and Amanda took off their skates. Cindy's mom talked to Carol Parton for another minute or so, then went with the girls out to the car.

On the way back to Cedar Terrace, the whispered discussion in the back seat was, again, about Mary Jo Green.

"Her ghost got us to come skating just like she did when she was alive," Amanda breathed, her eyes wide and solemn.

Cindy's voice raised. "I think somebody was jealous of her, I don't care what Mrs. Parton says."

Amanda's eyes cast a warning.

Sure enough, Cindy's mom asked, "Are you talking about Mary Jo Green again?"

"Yes," Cindy answered sullenly.

"It's a shame she didn't get to skate last year."

"It's a shame she's dead!"

"Right. So you stay away from that street corner like I told you to. And stop pestering people about her."

Cindy frowned at the back of her mother's head. She didn't care what the grownups told her, she was not going to give up until she had solved the mystery.

Chapter 13
Revelations

The Smallwood family were members of Grace Church. They attended services Sunday morning. It was the first time they'd gone since Mr. Smallwood had last been home in April, three months earlier. Because it was another hot day they dressed in lightweight summer clothes, Jennifer in a white cotton sundress with a tiny print of lavender blossoms, Mrs. Smallwood in a beige cotton suit. Mr. Smallwood wore a short-sleeved knit shirt and light-colored chinos, most unlike his usual business suit.

He gave the Smiths the day off and drove the Mercedes. Jennifer hadn't even been inside the car in a year and felt strange sitting on the gray leather seats. She refused to envision what the car might have been involved in.

They parked in the lot and approached the big brick building. People said hello and shook Mr. Smallwood's hand as they went inside and took their seats in the padded wooden pews. Jennifer was a little uncomfortable the whole service; she felt as if everyone was staring at her because she was there so seldom.

When the service was over they stood in line to shake hands with Reverend Jacobs, who asked them how they were. Jennifer was glad when they could take their leave. She still felt self-conscious.

They were in the parking lot, almost to their car, when someone shouted, "Jennifer! Hey!"

Startled, Jennifer looked around. Waving at her were Amanda and Cindy, who stood beside the Carter's blue van with Amanda's family. Amanda was dressed in pink Capri pants and tee shirt; Cindy wore denim shorts and a blue tee shirt, with those bandannas tied around her upper arms. Amanda's parents and little brother were also casually dressed.

Jennifer's mood became happy.

"Hello!" she called, smiling and waving back. "Dad, those are Cindy and Amanda, the two girls I met recently."

"Well, I'd like to meet them myself." He led the way past the next row of cars and down a little to reach the van.

"Mom, Dad," said Jennifer, "these are Mrs. Carter, Amanda Carter, her little brother Tayvon, and this is Cindy Buford. They're the girls I've been skating with this past week."

"How do you do?" said several people at once. Tayvon merely grinned, showing two missing front teeth.

"And I'm William Carter," said Amanda's father, smiling and sticking out his hand. Mr. Smallwood shook it. Mrs. Smallwood merely smiled, inclined her head to include everyone, and answered, "Pleased to meet you."

Mr. Smallwood said to the Carters, "It was very generous of you to take Jennifer to the roller rink. Thank you very much."

"You're welcome," said Mrs. Carter, "and thank you for taking our daughter and her friend to the ice rink last week."

"Oh, that was my wife's doing. I was out of town until Friday."

Jennifer pressed her lips together and fought to keep from laughing out loud. It was funny, her father giving her mother that credit, when Mrs. Smallwood had been so opposed to Jennifer's involvement with them.

"I'm glad they came along," he continued, "and I hope they do so again." He smiled directly at Amanda and Cindy. "Please come visit Jennifer at our house soon. It's good that she's met some people she has so much in common with."

Now Jennifer smothered a gasp. All they had in common was their curiosity about a dead woman. Then her father added, "I understand you're both skaters. Skating of all forms is a passion of Jennifer's."

Mrs. Carter nodded. "Yes, these two are always zipping around, though I think they like sidewalks better than indoors."

"Not any more, Mom," interposed Amanda. "Remember, we're taking lessons now?"

"Oh, are you?" Jennifer was surprised.

"Yes, at the roller rink, from Barbara McAllister. She gave us a semi-private lesson yesterday." Cindy spoke with recognizable pride.

Jennifer felt a sudden disappointment, as if she had been left out of something she really wanted to do. She tried not to let it show in her face. "Well, that's great. But you'll still come ice skating, won't you? Sometime next week?"

"Oh, sure. That was fun, too," said Amanda. But she wasn't smiling, and Cindy, looking sad, merely nodded. Jennifer remembered they had not done very well on ice.

"I guess we have to go," said Mr. Carter. "We have plans for this afternoon."

"Very nice to meet you all. I hope to see you again soon," said Mr. Smallwood.

"Same here."

The two groups separated to their vehicles and were soon in a line of cars turning from the parking lot onto Turnberry, the Carter's van just in front of the Smallwood's Mercedes.

"So those are your new friends, Jennifer," said her father. "I like them. Where do they go to school?"

"Murrayville Middle School, I guess. They both just moved in a couple of months ago. They live in Cedar Terrace."

"Yes, you told me. Well, I hope they do come over. The house seems awfully empty lately."

Jennifer noticed a slight wince on her mother's face. Ahead of them the Carters' van turned right into Cedar Terrace. The dark blue Mercedes headed on for Smallwood Lane and its namesake mansion.

Jennifer and her mother got out at the front door and went to the kitchen to begin lunch while Mr. Smallwood drove the car to the garage, just like Victor Smith always did.

They fixed the meal without Mrs. Smith's help for the first time in ages. It wasn't a lot of work, really. Mrs. Smallwood placed bread, lunchmeat, and cheese onto a silver serving tray, then opened a pre-packaged relish tray of pickles, olives, sliced carrots and celery. Jennifer sliced tomatoes and onions and shredded some lettuce. The two of them set the dining room table with china plates, crystal tea glasses, and silverware, and carried in the food.

Mr. Smallwood, meanwhile, came in and began preparing his own special blend of iced tea. He started water boiling on the stove. From the garden he had gathered fresh mint stalks. Now he crushed the mint and put it into a china teapot. He added four Earl Gray teabags and a couple of dashes of cinnamon spice. When the water boiled he poured it into the teapot and put on the lid so the mixture could steep for five minutes.

By the time the food was on the table, he was pouring the tea into a large silver pitcher three-quarters filled with ice. He smiled as he brought the pitcher to the sideboard of the dining room, then the silver ice container.

"This is going to be the best iced tea you've ever tried," he promised.

Everyone sat down, her parents at each end of the table, Jennifer along the side where she could face the window. She said the blessing over the food, something else that hadn't been done for a long time. Her parents began to make sandwiches. Jennifer sugared her tea and took a sip.

"Dad, this is wonderful!"

Mrs. Smallwood nodded her assent. "Oh, yes, Roger, where did you learn to make tea like this?"

"It's a European recipe," he answered, badly mimicking a British accent. Both the women laughed.

Jennifer's father joked during the meal, telling them about things that had happened on his latest extended business trip. He had traveled all over Europe finalizing contracts for his company, which purchased and transported machinery to clients around the world.

Mrs. Smallwood brought in little bowls of melon balls for dessert.

"I'd rather have ice cream," said Jennifer.

"This is much more healthy."

As he ate his dessert, Mr. Smallwood's manner grew serious and he stopped talking. Jennifer wondered what was wrong. Her stomach began to hurt. Was she about to get in trouble over something? Her mother seemed extremely sad, hardly raising her eyes from her bowl. When her father finished and wiped his mouth with a linen napkin, he looked positively grim

He said, "Jennifer, there's something we need to talk about."

Oh, no! What had she done? Maybe it wasn't her? Suddenly she thought of things like the blue car in the garage, and Mary Jo Green, and knew she didn't want to hear what he was about to say.

•••

"Your mother has something to tell you."

Mrs. Smallwood shook her head without raising it. "No, Roger, I can't talk about it. You tell her."

He took a deep breath. "Something very serious has happened to your mother. You remember when you asked me if I knew she hadn't driven in a year, and I said yes, I knew?"

Jennifer nodded, unable to speak. Her insides were trembling. What had her mother done! Was it what she thought? Please, no!

"Well . . . Jenn, your mother is going blind."

Jennifer was dumbfounded. This was not what she was expecting. Finally she managed a very weak, "What!" She looked wildly back and forth between her parents. "Blind! But then she couldn't have run into—I mean, she won't be able to see? Anything at all?"

"We don't know for certain. She has a condition where eyesight slowly fades away. Some people keep part of their vision for a while. Some never go completely blind. But she can't see as clearly as she used to. That's why . . ." Now her mother spoke.

"That's why I don't drive any more and don't go places. Nothing looks like it used to and I always feel a little lost. So I stay in the house, where everything is familiar and normal. And I have Victor drive me everywhere."

"When—when did you find out?"

"A little over a year ago in the spring. It was dark around the edges of my vision, and I could only see things up close. The ophthalmologist gave me some glasses, but they didn't help much, so I didn't wear them."

"Well, you—you have to go back and make him check your eyes again! Things could have changed in a year."

"I go all the time, when you're in school or ice skating practice. I just say I've been to the beauty salon or to some store."

Jennifer felt sick and afraid. The terrible things she had been thinking about her mother, when all the time she was losing her sight! Jennifer began crying.

"Oh, Jenn, please don't cry," begged her mother, and she started to sob along. "I'm so sorry. It was wrong of me not to tell you. But I didn't really want to believe it myself." She stood and moved around to a chair beside Jennifer, then sat down next to her and put her arm around her.

"And I'm so sorry I tried to control what you did so much. I felt like I couldn't protect you any more unless I knew exactly where you were and who was around you. I wanted to make sure nothing ever happened to you." Tears were running freely down Mrs. Smallwood's face now. Jennifer leaned against her shoulder. Jennifer's father came and placed his arms around the two of them. "I know we should have told you before, but Lorraine wanted to wait in case it would turn out not to be true. But there's no denying, it's growing worse. That's why I've arranged to be around all the time now."

Jennifer's father continued, "It took a long time to train my overseas replacement. Now I feel confident I can take a local desk position with the company. It can even be part-time if I decide that's necessary. My biggest job right now is looking after my family."

He gave Jennifer his handkerchief so she could blow her nose. Her mother took a table napkin and dried her own eyes.

Jennifer said, "I can't believe the awful things I thought were going on."

He nodded. "People jump to the worst conclusions when they don't know what's really happening. It's our fault for leaving you in the dark."

"Roger, please," protested Mrs. Smallwood, "you know I hate puns."

Jennifer and her father stared at her mother a moment. She was making a joke about her blindness! They both burst into laughter, and she laughed along with them.

They stayed like that awhile longer, holding hands and leaning against each other. Finally Mrs. Smallwood straightened in her chair and stood. "Well, I don't know about you two, but I'm tired of looking at these dirty dishes."

"Yes, let's clean them up."

They cleared the table and washed the china and silver by hand; her mother washing, Jennifer and her father drying and putting away. When they were done her father said, "Who feels like going to a movie?"

Jennifer glanced at her mother. "Oh, I'd love to! But can she see well enough?"

"I can see a movie screen just fine if I wear those ugly glasses," said Mrs. Smallwood. "I guess I'll have to from now on."

"I'll check the paper to see what's playing," said her father.

"I can check on-line," offered Jennifer. "I can even reserve tickets for a show."

"You can do all that? I want to watch."

They went up to Jennifer's room. She sat in front of her computer and nudged the mouse to make the screen appear.

"Who's that girl on your wallpaper?" asked her father.

"Girl on the wallpaper?" asked her mother, looking around at the familiar floral pattern of Jennifer's walls.

"The picture on her computer screen when no program is running. It's called 'wallpaper,'" said Jennifer's father.

Jennifer answered, "That's T-Bird, a girl singer and rapper. She's very popular right now." T-Bird rolled across the screen smiling, wearing bandanna armbands and blue jeans and, on her feet, in-line roller skates.

"She certainly does dress strangely," commented Mrs. Smallwood.

Next to roll across the screen was Ronnie Haven, the Junior Men's Singles champion. He and his partner Laurie Sokolsky were also the Junior Pairs champions.

"I know who that is!" exclaimed Mrs. Smallwood, smiling.

Jennifer went on-line and found the local movie schedules. They finally chose a comedy. Jennifer reserved three tickets for a show starting an hour later. Then she logged off.

They left for the movie, Roger Smallwood driving, Lorraine Smallwood appearing rather self-conscious in lavender metal-rimmed glasses that Jennifer didn't remember ever seeing before. Jennifer sat in the back seat of the Mercedes, wearing a white sweater against the air-conditioning in the car and movie theater.

The movie was funny, and they all laughed a lot. Then they went to their favorite restaurant again for dinner, all in a very good mood.

But driving home, Jennifer felt sad about her mother's deteriorating physical condition. What else might go wrong? Did she have a disease? Jennifer imagined her mother's whole body wasting away, not just her eyesight. Her body might grow thin and skeletal and her pale blonde hair might all fall out. Would Jennifer get it too? How would she ice skate then, or study for school, or go for walks?

Then she felt ashamed. Mary Jo Green had gone for a walk and she'd died. That was a lot worse than just going blind. And there was something she needed to do about that.

Back home, she waited until her mother had gone upstairs to get ready for bed. Then she approached her father. He was in his office, going over some papers, when she came into the room and sat down hesitantly in one of the big chairs. "Want something, Jennifer?"

She hesitated, hoping he wouldn't ask too many questions.

"Dad, could you get something for me? A car's license plate number?"

Chapter 14
Disappointments

Cindy arrived home from church to surprise visitors.

She and Amanda were planning to go swimming that afternoon. But as the van turned into Cedar Terrace, she noticed a familiar 1957 green-and-white Chevrolet parked in one of the four visitor spots.

She leaned her head back against the seat as if in pain. "Oh no," she muttered. "There's his old car that he restored, I'll bet he's got big mouth Peter with him, and Linda will be smiling that sick pathetic look she always gives me."

"What? Who's here?" whispered Amanda.

"My father and his family. Now I have to listen to Peter screaming." She thought of something else. She sat up and clapped her hand over her mouth. "Oh, no! They can't be here to take me back to Baltimore!"

Mr. and Mrs. Carter looked around. "What is it?"

"My father's here," Cindy answered dejectedly.

"Well, that's nice," smiled Mrs. Carter. "It's good that he came to visit."

Amanda said, "He might take her back to Baltimore!"

"Oh, dear."

Mr. Carter slowed the van to a stop in front of Cindy's house. "Remember, we're leaving for the pool in an hour."

Cindy opened the side door and got out. "I probably won't get to go," she commented sourly. Then she looked at those concrete steps. She did not want to climb them, but she did, slowly. The door was locked, so she knocked instead of fishing for her key. Her mother opened it.

"Come in, Cindy. Your father and his family have come to visit."

"I'm kind of hungry so I'll just stay in the kitchen and eat, okay?"

"How about I bring you a ham sandwich into the living room. Go on back now."

Cindy sighed. Mom wasn't going to let her hide in the kitchen. *Mom* was going to hide in the kitchen.

Cindy went down the hall and turned left into the small living room. Its walls and carpet were a dull beige color. It was furnished with the old living room set from their house back in Cherry Hill. The shabby green sofa was backed up to the picture window with the green armchair catty-corner to it and the scratched brown coffee table in front of it. The wooden rocker that had belonged to Cindy's grandmother sat near the doorway.

Sitting on the couch was Linda Buford, Cindy's stepmother. Linda looked tired and hot; her frizzy, blondish hair was damp around her face and her eyes had circles under them. Beside her slept Peter, mercifully quiet. Even though he was almost a year old, Peter woke up a lot and had probably kept his mother up half the night. In the month since Cindy had seen him, Peter seemed to have grown a lot longer and heavier.

"Hello, Cindy," said Linda, smiling as if her teeth hurt.

Tom Buford was in the armchair. His dark hair was combed in its usual pompadour style. People said he looked a little like Elvis Presley, so he tried to copy the famous star, even though he had been only ten years old when Elvis died.

Tom smiled and stood up. He was lots shorter than Elvis had been. "Hi, Cindy. We've missed you, Honey." He held out his arms for a hug.

Cindy found herself glad to see her father. She ran across the room and hugged him. Then she kissed Linda on the cheek.

Her father motioned her to sit beside him in the armchair. She had to take the armrest because, like Elvis, her father was getting kind of fat. He put his arm around her and she leaned back against him; it was not the most comfortable position.

"So, are you having a good time this summer?" asked Linda. She actually sounded as if she cared.

"Yes, lots of fun."

"I hear you've made some friends."

"A couple of girls who live nearby." She squirmed, trying not to fall off the chair arm.

"That's good," commented her father.

"And you're taking roller skating lessons?" continued Linda.

"I took one yesterday, with Amanda."

There was a pause. Cindy's mom brought in a sandwich and a glass of juice. She put them on the coffee table and went to sit in the rocker. Cindy slid down to the rug to eat her lunch.

Her father coughed, and Cindy knew the pleasantries were over. "Your mom says you want to come live with her."

Cindy nodded, her mouth full. She kept her eyes on her plate.

"You know that I can't afford to pay any more money for child support."

Cindy swallowed and took a drink of apple juice.

"That's why you live with me, because your mom can't support you either."

Cindy took another bite and chewed vigorously.

"So I don't see how we could manage for you to—"

Cindy had thought of several ways they could afford it. She swallowed again and told him, "You could move out of that expensive apartment and into a cheap place with only two bedrooms. Then you'd have more money."

"That place is near my job." Her father repaired and restored old cars at a garage that had been in Fells Point for a long time. "And cheap apartments are full of drug addicts and lowlifes. I have to keep my family safe."

Cindy carefully kept her face expressionless. "Move to Murrayville, where life is safer." She stiffened her shoulders and head against the onslaught she knew was coming.

"Look, I don't need any lip out of you! I do the best I can for my family, nobody can say I don't, and I don't need some little upstart to tell me how to manage! You just better learn—"

Her father was interrupted by a wail from the couch. His shouts had awakened Peter. Linda glared at the man. "Did you have to wake him up!" she demanded. Her expression changed so she looked ready to cry as the baby climbed screaming into her lap.

Now, on top of her father's lectures, Cindy had to listen to Peter bawl.

The toddler's head was on his mother's shoulder, his hair much shorter than hers but of the same dark blond color and frizzy texture. Linda rubbed circles on his back with the palm of her hand, trying to calm his yells.

Tom Buford sighed sharply in exasperation. Cindy glanced sideways at her mother. Valerie Buford's face was neutral, except for the way she narrowed her eyes to slits at Cindy. She was rocking in short, quick bursts.

After a couple of minutes, Peter's shrieks subsided to sobs. Linda reached into the diaper bag that sat on the floor beside the couch and pulled out a small plastic baby bottle. Peter took it and held it in his mouth, his eyes squeezed shut as he drank. Soon, though, he opened his eyes and looked around. He began to grin with the bottle's nipple smashed between his tiny four front teeth. At sight of Cindy, he squealed with pleasure and dropped the bottle so it bounced on the couch and onto the floor. He wriggled from his mother's arms and slid down to the carpet. Holding the coffee table for support, he toddled around to Cindy, lurched onto her, and wrapped his arms around her neck.

"Tinny! Tinny!" he yelled. That was what he always called her because he couldn't say her name right. Cindy shoved her plate back from the edge of the coffee table with her right hand, and with her left hand tried to loosen Peter's grip on her neck so she could breathe.

"Hello, Brat," she said, trying to frown, twisting her lips so they wouldn't grin. "He's getting around better," she said to Linda.

"He's really missed you," her stepmother said.

Cindy wanted to answer, I *haven't missed him!* But little happy feelings were going through her stomach, and her cheek was tingling where his pressed against hers.

She lay back on the rug and sat Peter on her stomach, then held his hands and began bouncing him up and down the way he liked. He chortled with laughter. After a couple of minutes they were both tired; he lay down on her stomach, his head on her chest, and began to suck his thumb.

"Take that thing out of there," she said, pulling his thumb from his mouth. Instead of crying, he grinned and tried to stick the wet thumb into Cindy's mouth. "Yuck!" she shouted. He giggled out loud.

Meanwhile the adults were smiling and laughing quietly.

"Hey, Petey!" said Tom Buford. "You're a bad boy. You know that, Petey?"

Peter began prying at Cindy's pressed lips, trying to pull them open so he could insert his thumb. Cindy put up with it for about a minute, then she put her arms around Peter and rolled sideways so he was lying on the floor next to her. She loosened her arms, slid them out, and sat up. "I've got to finish my lunch." She scooted back over to the coffee table.

Peter crawled to the table and pushed uncertainly to his feet. He found his balance, ran to the doorway, and then into the hall.

"He can walk now?" Cindy was surprised.

Linda was up and after him in a shot. She came back into the room with him struggling in her arms. "He just started a few days ago."

Cindy felt deprived and angry that she hadn't been around to see her little brother take his first steps. She sulked as she stuffed a bite of sandwich into her mouth.

"We could take him down to the basement to run around, or into the back yard," Cindy's mom suggested.

"Good idea." Linda found Peter's shoes in the diaper bag and put them on his feet. Then she carried him after Cindy's mom, down the steps to the basement. Cindy finished eating and went to look out the window. She saw them in the tiny fenced back yard, Peter running across the thin grass, the two women sitting in old folding aluminum chairs.

Cindy's father still sat in the armchair. She could tell he was trying to figure out how to say something. She began to leave the room with her plate.

"Cindy, wait. I need to talk to you."

Cindy put the plate back down and went to sit on the couch. She crossed her arms and stared at her knees. She thought, *Don't say it, please don't say it.*

"Look, I know it's not easy living in the city. I miss Cherry Hill where we used to live. Back there we could go for a walk and not worry about anybody bothering us. And in Baltimore, nobody can go out without a baseball bat and a machine gun."

Cindy had never had a weapon, but now was no time to say she could take care of herself in Baltimore.

He went on, "But where we live now, I can take a bus to work so Linda can use the car if she needs to do errands or take Peter somewhere. Your school is just down the street from where we live."

Cindy groaned quietly. The elementary school she had attended in Baltimore was dirty and full of rough kids, just like the city streets. And she knew the middle school she would have to go to in the fall was going to be even worse.

Please don't say it, she begged silently.

"I know it's not great," her father continued. "I just—can't come up with any more money right now. And the truth is, if you and your mother want to change the situation, she'll have to pay her lawyer to go to court. She can't afford that. She can't even pay for your clothes and food if you live here with her. I just barely have enough when you stay at my place."

Cindy couldn't resist a smart remark. "So you're saying I should run away and live on my own."

"No, I am not saying that and you know it! Why do you always have to—" He stopped and took a couple of deep breaths before he went on. "You already know what I'm saying. You have to come back to Baltimore the end of August, before school starts."

He'd said it.

Cindy had an awful sensation in her stomach, and she felt like her arms and legs couldn't move. She wanted to slide down onto the couch and fall asleep like a helpless baby, to curl into a ball and never wake up.

He stood up. "Sorry I yelled at you earlier. You know, I just can't seem to make you understand." He loitered uncertainly. "I'm not just being mean. I want to see you back." He walked over and kissed her on the forehead, this look on his face like he hoped she could read his mind or something. But she kept her own face blank.

He finally went to the hallway and down the basement stairs. Soon Cindy heard his voice out in the back yard with the others.

She closed her eyes. She didn't feel like crying or sleeping or anything. She just felt like—like she didn't exist any more.

After a couple of minutes, she went to the telephone in the kitchen and called Amanda. Mrs. Carter answered the phone.

"May I speak to Amanda?"

"We're just going out the door to go swimming."

"Can I still come along? I only have to get my swimsuit and a towel and I'm ready."

"Sure, we'll be by for you in five minutes."

Cindy got her old red swimsuit and the big beach towel with the holes in it, then put on her flip-flops and hurried downstairs to the basement. She opened the sliding door into the back yard.

Peter was sitting on a blanket in the too-tall grass, trying to put dandelions into his mouth, while Linda sat next to him, grabbing everything from his hands. Tom Buford was in one of the two chairs, her mother in the other one; they were sitting a good distance apart from each other on the tiny concrete patio. They were speaking, probably about Cindy, without ever looking at each other.

Cindy did not want to go back into that tiny expensive Baltimore apartment that was smaller than this house and that didn't have a yard or a friend nearby for her to play with. Four people crowded into that little place even as much as it cost, and Cindy's bedroom was not much bigger than a closet, and that was mean because Peter had a bigger room than she did, which let her know which kid they liked better.

Yet Cindy realized Peter was the only one she'd really miss.

"I'm leaving now," she announced. "I'm supposed to go swimming and they're coming to pick me up."

Her mother looked exasperated. "Cindy—"

"I'll only be a couple of hours."

Her father rose from his chair. "It's time for us to be getting back too. Come on, Linda."

Linda's expression turned sad. Cindy knew Linda didn't like that ugly city, and this little back yard must be the closest she'd been to a farm field in a long time.

Cindy closed the sliding patio door and turned her back on all of them. She ascended the stairs to the front door and out to where the Carters' van was waiting.

Chapter 15
Dangers

Monday was three hundred sixty-four days since Mary Jo's death. One day short of a whole year.

"Tuesday is the calendar date when she died, not today," argued Amanda.

"That's not what Carol Parton said. She said Monday is a year. That's today."

The two girls were in the basement, finally awake at one p.m. after a late night of gaming and television. Cindy's mother almost hadn't let Amanda spend the night because Cindy had run out on Sunday afternoon. But Cindy finally talked her into it.

"Don't ghosts always appear three hundred and sixty-five days later? Today is three hundred sixty-four days, not a whole year."

"What if it's a leap year? That's three hundred sixty-six days. Besides, she appeared a bunch of times last week before the year was up."

"Yeah. Well, maybe she came around last week because the anniversary was coming and she wanted somebody to catch her killer."

"Maybe she's around every day. She just doesn't talk to people most of the time."

"I just hope she comes today."

•••

Jennifer Smallwood had just gotten back from her regular dance and skating lessons, tired and ready for a nap. Her father had stayed home to get some telephone work done. As she was dragging her skate bag up the stairs to her room the door into her father's study opened.

"Jenn, I've got that information you wanted." He held out a piece of paper.

Jennifer left her skate bag on a step and hurried back down, exhaustion replaced by eagerness.

She took the computer printout, said, "Thank you very much, Father," and gave it a quick scan.

It was a disappointment.

"This says that the owner of that license plate is named Jonathan Leifer." Big deal. He was the guy who owned the house next door to Mary Jo's. Why shouldn't the red car from its garage belong to him too?

"Is that what you needed to know?"

She tried to conceal her disappointment with a smile. "Yes, this is just great. Thank you so much." She was turning toward the stairs again when she read something else on the page. It made her stop dead still and gasp.

"He owns another car—a dark blue Lincoln Continental!"

"Is that important?"

She grabbed her father around the neck and kissed him hard on the cheek. "More important than anything!" she shouted, and ran back up the steps.

"Don't forget to take your skates up," he called.

"Oh, yeah." She hurried down and clutched the heavy bag, then sped back up as if it weighed almost nothing.

She grabbed her princess telephone and dialed Cindy's number.

•••

Cindy ran up the basement stairs to the kitchen. "This better not be a telemarketer." She lifted the telephone receiver. "Hello?"

"Cindy, this is Jennifer. I found out who owns that red car. It's that man named Jonathan Leifer who owns that house next to Mary Jo's, and guess what? He owns a dark blue Continental!"

"A what?"

"A Lincoln Continental. A big dark car. Like the one that hit Mary Jo!"

"Oh, wow!"

Jennifer heard some whispering from Cindy's end.

"Who are you talking to?"

"Amanda. She spent the night here last night." More whispering.

Jennifer felt a pang as she realized no friend had ever slept over at her own house. She was suddenly very lonely. "Are you doing anything today?"

"We just decided we're going blading. Then we're going back to Mary Jo's neighborhood to see what we can find out now that we know more about that Leifer guy. Do you want to come along?"

"Sure. Look, I'm really tired and I have to take a nap first. I'll be up in about an hour."

"That'll be after two o'clock. Call us when you do get up."

"I will. 'Bye!"

Jennifer hung up her phone and lay back on her bed. Why would Mary Jo's neighbor have run her down? Was that why he didn't live in the house any more? And surely the police would have found out that the man who lived next door to the dead lady owned a car like the one that hit her! They would have already checked it out, wouldn't they?

Jennifer's thoughts were growing fuzzy. They trailed off as she fell into a deep doze, and then to sleep.

•••

Cindy and Amanda got into an excited discussion.

"So maybe that was the owner who was in the house when we were talking to Mrs. Grant next door," said Cindy.

"Yeah, but why would he stay inside and then run away?"

"Because he had something to hide! He must have overheard us asking about Mary Jo and that got him worried and he drove off in a hurry when he thought we were gone."

"Jennifer says he owns a dark blue car. Isn't it funny the police didn't question him? There wasn't even anything in the paper about him."

"Yeah, you'd think some reporter would ask him if Mary Jo was a good neighbor or how he felt about the dangerous streets or something." Cindy paused as a new thought entered her mind. "You know what?"

"What?"

"Did you see the car that Jennifer's family was driving on Sunday? It was dark blue."

"Maybe Jennifer's father ran Mary Jo down."

"Don't be silly!" Cindy exclaimed, but there was doubt on her face.

"So when are we going to Evergreen Woods?"

"When Jennifer gets up from her nap in an hour."

"But the accident was at 5:30 so it wouldn't do any good to go out earlier. That's the time of day Mary Jo appeared to each of us."

Cindy shrugged. "We'll go blading in the park to kill time. Now let's go eat; I'm hungry."

They ate cold cereal, then Amanda helped Cindy with chores.

•••

Jennifer opened woozy eyes and looked at the numbers on her clock. She sat up with a gasp. It was two-thirty. She was late!

She was practicing harder at both her skating and her dancing to please her father, so she was extra tired. That must be why she had slept so long. From her dresser she took out khaki shorts and a pink tee shirt, so she could match Amanda. Then she found some scarves to tie around her arms so she'd match Cindy. The scarves were see-through silk, one green, one pink, but she didn't have any bandannas.

She put on white socks and took out her in-line roller skates, helmet, knee and elbow pads. She carried them all downstairs and left them by the front door before going into the kitchen for a snack.

Mrs. Smith was cooking something in a pot on the stove and Mrs. Smallwood was at the table, drinking a cup of coffee. When Jennifer walked into the room, Mrs. Smallwood's eyes narrowed slightly.

"Why are you dressed that way?"

"It's very stylish right now."

"Like that girl roller skating across your computer screen. Well, nice to see you up, anyway. We're going out soon."

"What? Where?"

"To Silver Spring. Your father wants to see that new skating costume. He hasn't met this seamstress yet."

"But I have plans for the afternoon."

"Plans?" Now Mrs. Smallwood had that look where she had to approve everything Jennifer did.

"I'm meeting Cindy and Amanda. We're going to sidewalk skate."

"I'm sure that's something that can wait."

"But it can't! Today is the day when . . ." Her voice trailed off. It was not a good idea to mention Mary Jo and how she had been killed crossing the street a year earlier. That would probably make her mother say she couldn't go on the streets at all. "When we said we'd get together," Jennifer finished lamely.

"Well, you can see them when we get back, or change it until tomorrow. I don't want to disappoint your father."

Mrs. Smith put the lid onto the pot and left the room.

"He won't be disappointed," Jennifer insisted. "We can go and see that stupid costume tomorrow!"

"Jennifer! Don't you ever speak to me like that!" Mrs. Smallwood was now glaring in the same old way as before Mr. Smallwood was home.

Jennifer controlled her voice but returned the hateful look. She was getting tired of being pushed around by this woman. "I'm sorry for speaking unpleasantly. But I am tired of everything I do revolving around ice skating, and never having any time to spend by myself away from it. And you know Dad agrees with me. In fact, he probably wouldn't mind going to see the costume without me."

Her mother's expression was triumphant. "No, he is looking forward to seeing you model it. He expects to have you along. If you don't believe me, go ask him."

"I will certainly do that." Jennifer turned on her heel and hurried to her father's study, waited till he got off the phone, then asked, "Dad, do I really have to come along while you go see that new costume? I want to meet Cindy and Amanda to go blading."

"Haven't you had enough skating for one day? I'd love to see this new costume on you. Your mother says it's a real beauty."

"I've tried it on a bunch of times already. I'd like to have some fun instead."

"Tell you what—when we get back you may go meet your friends and skate with them until it's almost dark. How's that?"

"Dad, that's too late! Mary Jo won't be—" She stopped.

"Who's Mary Jo, another friend? You haven't mentioned her before."

"Sort of," she muttered. "I met her once."

"Jennifer, hold your head up and speak clearly as your mother has taught you to do."

Jennifer lifted her chin. "She lives in Evergreen Woods. We were going to meet her today."

"Well, I'm sorry to spoil your plans. Why don't you call your friends and apologize, and tell them you'll be late." It was an order, not a question. He turned in his swivel chair and studied the paintings on the wall behind his desk the way he always did when he was finished with a discussion.

Jennifer forced herself to walk, not stomp, to the door, then to close it softly behind her instead of slamming it. She went upstairs to her room and sat on the end of her bed, where she stared straight ahead at her reflection in the mirror. She was so angry that she forgot to call Cindy and Amanda and tell them she would be very late.

When her mother called for her, she practically marched downstairs and out to the car.

As she sat in the back seat of the BMW she thought to herself, *I am not going to talk to them unless they ask me something directly. I am not going to enjoy this. I am going to make them as miserable as they are making me.*

All the silent way down and back, Jennifer had the immense satisfaction of feeling that she was achieving her goal and making her parents very sorry they had forced her to come.

But not as sorry as she herself was, because the whole time all she could think about was Cindy and Amanda and what they might be finding out.

● ● ●

The girls were distracted from their chores by a pillow fight while they were trying to change the sheets on Cindy's bed. Then they played hide-and-seek in her mother's bedroom. Finally they had the dirty sheets in the washing machine and came up to load the dishwasher.

Amanda looked at the clock. "It's almost three!"

"Let's go call Jennifer on the phone."

But an elderly lady's voice answered the telephone and informed Cindy that the Smallwood family was out for the afternoon.

Cindy hung up the phone. "What do we do now?"

"We go without her."

Chapter 16
The Deadly Corner

Blading up Turnberry to the park and back down again was usually a lot of fun. Today, however, stopping for ice cream and skating along the paths was just passing the time until they could look for Mary Jo.

A little after five o'clock, Cindy and Amanda were waiting in front of Rose Witcrest's house. Cindy spoke anxiously.

"You're sure she'll come out?"

"This is when she walks Tootsie and Mitzi on the days when she's feeling okay. It was this time I met her last week."

"Does she know it was this day a year ago Mary Jo was killed?"

"She knows it was a year ago, but I don't know about the same day."

Just then the gate in the picket fence began to open; the top of a white head of hair appeared just above it. Finally the gate was completely open. Rose Witcrest came walking out with two fluffy white dogs.

Cindy gaped. "Wow, she's really funny looking."

The tiny lady was dressed in a cowgirl outfit of a strange color. Her matching blouse and skirt were bright orange and trimmed with white fringe. On her feet and covering much of her short, bowed legs were white cowgirl boots.

The dogs wore matching orange bows on the tops of their heads.

Just as before, Tootsie was on hind legs trying to reach Amanda, and Rose was dragging on Tootsie's leash while seeming not to notice anyone. Mitzi was trotting along as if there were no one in the world but herself. They reached the

sidewalk parallel to the street and Cindy and Amanda skated up beside them. "Hello, Rose," said Amanda.

Rose looked around. "Nice to see you, Amanda. Who's your friend?"

"This is my neighbor Cindy Buford."

"How do you do, Mrs. Witcrest?" Cindy asked.

"Quite well, Miss Buford. What brings the two of you out today?" There was a knowing look in her eye, as if she didn't need to ask the question.

Amanda began, "Oh, we just thought we'd—"

"Mary Jo was killed a year ago," said Cindy, "and we were wondering if you'd heard anything or found out anything about her killer?"

"Oh, not I. You girls probably know a great deal more than I could tell you."

Despite the lady's short steps, they were moving along at a rapid pace. Amanda answered, "Well, we found out that Mary Jo's neighbor Jonathan Leifer owns a car like the kind that killed her."

Rose Witcrest's expression was one of genuine surprise. "Really? I thought he had a red car. He used to bother her all the time and even spied on her. Wanted her to go out on dates with him. I think she was sorry she had to live next door to him."

Cindy and Amanda exchanged a look. "No kidding," said Cindy. "He was stalking her?"

"I don't know that I would call it that. But she was very glad when she found out he was buying a house in Baltimore."

"Yes, he owns one there," supplied Amanda. "I wonder why this one never sold?"

Said Cindy, "Mrs. Grant said she'd never seen a realtor there."

"There must have been one sometime or there wouldn't be a sign."

"You two get around, don't you?" commented Rose.

The duplex of interest was just ahead on their left, and they couldn't help but stare. Mrs. Grant was sitting on the porch steps of the right-hand unit, the one that had been Mary Jo's, while her two children rode tricycles on the driveway. "Hello," she greeted the girls. "Hello, Mrs. Witcrest." Mrs. Grant was smiling in a fake manner. Brandon and Karen stopped pedaling and stared as they went past.

Rose bobbed her head. "Good evening," she said pleasantly. Cindy and Amanda answered, "Hi," Cindy rather absent-mindedly. She was concentrating on the left half of the duplex, the part Jonathan Leifer owned, and looking for those telltale movements of the curtains, but she didn't see anything.

Then the duplex was behind them; Cindy kept watching back over her shoulder. The two kids started pedaling again and Mrs. Grant went back to looking at a magazine.

Cindy, Amanda, and Rose hadn't gone much farther when the annoying fat kid Cindy had had the run-in with appeared across the street, standing next to the huge oak tree. "Hey, stupid old lady!" he taunted. "I hope those dogs eat you for supper." Amanda made a face at him.

Then he did a double-take at Cindy. "Mom!" He ran toward his house. "There's that JD that beat me up!" He disappeared inside his front door.

"What's he talking about?" asked Amanda.

"I have no idea," answered Cindy.

Rose merely chuckled. "That's our old friend Billy Bob Lawson." Cindy wondered if the lady knew what had happened.

A woman in a business suit and apron, black high heels on her feet, came glaring onto the Lawson front porch. She wasn't even as tall as her overweight son. They started after Rose's group, he pointing hard and talking fast. He was jumping up and down with anger and excitement; they left the porch and came up to the street. His grim mother was marching along like a drill sergeant, shouting something unclear.

"This place is always a circus," commented Rose. "It's best to just ignore everyone."

"That's what I'm doing," answered Cindy.

The dogs led the way. Just ahead loomed the fatal intersection of Turnberry Avenue and Smallwood Lane.

And on the other side, someone was rushing toward them down the sidewalk.

•••

The interminable afternoon was over. Jennifer was finally free to join the others. Wearing her helmet, she ran through the orchard with her in-line skates slung over her shoulder, not bothering with knee or elbow pads.

She did not intend to go through the woods. She stayed near her own

driveway, and where it joined Smallwood Lane, sat down on the grass and put on her skates. She got up and skated past the ranch style homes that lined Smallwood Lane. Moving swiftly, she jumped driveways and dodged toys that children had left behind. Once she had to brake to a complete stop as a car turned into a driveway just ahead of her. When it was barely past the sidewalk she was on her way again.

Ahead was that corner, the one where she had stood the week before, so sure her mother had caused Mary Jo's death. Jennifer knew something would happen today, and she wanted to be there when it did.

She reached the corner. There were Cindy and Amanda across the street, coming up the sidewalk to the intersection. They saw her; they waved. Someone was with them, a really strange-looking old lady. Jennifer had seen her before, a bunch of times. That must be Rose Witcrest. And she was walking two dogs. One of them must have been Mary Jo's, the dog she was looking for in the woods that time she spoke to Jennifer. It gave Jennifer an eerie feeling, almost as if Mary Jo were nearby and about to speak to her again . . .

Jennifer barely hesitated to glance both ways up and down Turnberry. She saw nothing coming and started across the street.

"Look out! Stop!" someone shouted, and she almost screamed in fright.

•••

"Look, it's Jennifer," said Amanda. "She's in a hurry."

They watched her start across the street.

She's not waiting long enough, thought Cindy, looking to the right toward the curve where Turnberry disappeared. There was no traffic coming from that direction. She looked to the left, toward Cedar Terrace and the library.

She saw a car.

It was a very dark blue. It was very large.

And it was coming very fast.

"Jennifer, no!" she screamed. She began frantically waving her arms. "There's a car coming!"

Amanda glanced left and saw the vehicle. "Stay back! You'll get hit!"

Just behind them, Rose Witcrest murmured, "Oh, my Lord. Oh, please don't let another girl get hit by a car here. I couldn't stand it."

The car was closer. It was almost to the intersection.

Now Jennifer saw the car. Her face filled with horror as she tried to dig in her heels to put on her brakes. But she was going too fast and she began to skid across the center yellow line.

Jennifer and the car were going to get to the same spot at the same time. One of them was going to knock the other out of the way. It was not hard to imagine which would get knocked down and which would keep going.

Cindy's voice was one long scream. Amanda wasn't able to make a sound. They both knew that, right in front of them, their friend Jennifer Smallwood was going to die just the same way Mary Jo Green did.

Suddenly Cindy saw someone else in the street.

It was Mary Jo Green, solid and real-looking. Her dress and high heels glowed almost an iridescent blue, and her bouffant hairdo seemed to catch fire in the blaze from the sun that hung low in the sky far to Cindy's right. Cindy was almost blinded, whether by the beauty of Mary Jo's appearance or by the bright sun shining onto Turnberry she wasn't sure. She wished she could see Mary Jo's bright green eyes again.

But Mary Jo stood sideways to Cindy, looking at the car rushing toward her. There was a strange, grim expression on her face, as if she were going into battle. Then Mary Jo's back was to Cindy and she was facing Jennifer. Mary Jo did something with her arms so her elbows stuck out to the sides. Then her elbows immediately disappeared from sight as her arms straightened to the front.

Cindy saw Jennifer suddenly thrown across the street. Mary Jo had shoved her so hard she landed on her back on the white concrete sidewalk.

Then Mary Jo was facing the car again. Its wheels screeched as it put on its brakes. Cindy could see the driver's profile, a man, his hair dark but graying, his nose sharp with a hump in it, and his face set in an expression of disbelief and horror.

Everything that went on took only fractions of a second. Cindy couldn't believe she could see so many things happening so clearly. And she didn't believe what she saw next.

The car went right through Mary Jo. It fishtailed and struck the opposite curb, ran up onto the concrete, and glanced off the fire hydrant near the corner.

Liquid began spreading from the bottom of the hydrant and onto the street. And the car kept moving.

Cindy heard screaming that was not her own. Her eyes began darting around, trying to take everything in. Jennifer was lying on the sidewalk across the street. Her head extended to the right and her legs pointed left, except the left knee was bent somehow outward toward Cindy, and the left leg, in-line skate still on, was down where the gutter would be if there was one.

The fat boy—Billy Bob?—and his mother were on the sidewalk in front of the advancing blue car. Mrs. Lawson was trying to run backward, her arms waving erratically, her mouth open. She tripped and fell onto the grass. The boy had already fallen on the concrete. He was crying, desperately crawling on his hands and knees away from the advancing car.

The car never reached them. Suddenly it stopped. The driver regained control, noisily backed off the curb, sped squealing down Turnberry, and disappeared around the curve.

It all took moments, yet it seemed like hours. Cindy stared across the blacktop at Jennifer where she lay with her back on the sidewalk and leg in the street. She was not moving. Cindy shoved to the curb and was about to skate across the road.

But there stood Mary Jo. Her eyes were that green neon color and her dress shone almost as brightly. "Stay back!" she shouted. "Don't cross!"

Cindy stopped and backed up. Beside her, Amanda did the same. Cindy wondered what Amanda had been doing for the past few seconds. To Cindy's left a couple of cars slowed down and came to a stop, the one in front just a few inches short of Mary Jo. Its driver, an elderly man, got out and rushed across the street to check on Jennifer. The next driver, a woman, was talking into a cellphone.

"This is just what happened when Mary Jo was hit," said Rose's elderly voice. Cindy realized the dogs were in a frenzy of barking.

Mary Jo's pale face now glowed like a brilliant moon and her mouth, redder than blood, was moving. Her arms were stretched out toward Cindy and Amanda. No one else seemed to see her.

"The car!" she demanded. "Did you see the license plate? Did you see the driver?"

"Yes," Cindy nodded, barely able to move her lips.

"We did," Amanda answered at the same time, her voice barely audible.

"Who are you talking to?" asked Rose.

Mary Jo's colors intensified. Her outstretched hands formed fists. She was like a statue of brilliant, streaming metals, filled with dynamite that was about to explode. Cindy wanted to cover her eyes but was paralyzed with fear.

Yet the dead woman's face turned sad, and her hands dropped limp at her sides. When she spoke again, the sound of her voice was like leaves falling from a tree.

"It's over," she said. Her image began to waver, the colors to grow dilute, to fade as if a rapid twilight were descending on everything.

Then she said "Goodbye," and it was like water evaporating from a puddle. What was left of her faded away into nothing. Like a cloud disappearing as the sunset darkened, she dissipated and was gone.

Cindy stood spellbound. In the part of the street where Mary Jo had been was a line of stopped cars that kept growing longer toward the library two blocks on the left. From the right appeared a growing backup of more stopped cars. Across the street lay Jennifer in a pink top and khaki shorts, half on, half off the sidewalk.

Chapter 17
The Hospital

Mrs. Buford found a spot in the parking lot. Cindy opened her passenger-side door and tried to jump out even before the car had stopped moving.

"You just wait like you're supposed to, young lady. I don't need you getting hit by a car too."

Cindy gritted her teeth and waited for her mother to open her own door before getting out.

Amanda exited the back seat. Cindy had almost forgotten she had come along. They all locked their doors and started across the still-warm asphalt toward the big brick building, lit up against the dark summer night with the words "Fern Oak Regional Hospital." They were going specifically toward the red and white sign that said "Emergency Room."

Amanda whispered to Cindy, "Are you all right? You haven't said anything the whole way here."

After an angry pause, Cindy whispered back, "I feel like it's all my fault."

"Why?"

"Because I'm the one who told her to come and meet us there."

"She would have come anyway."

"No, she wouldn't. If I hadn't called Jennifer, she would have stayed home and still be safe. And I'm the one who told her about Mary Jo Green and about the blue car and—"

"She found some of that stuff out on her own. Remember, Mary Jo appeared to her too."

They were hanging back so Mrs. Buford couldn't hear. Now Cindy's mother reached the sliding glass doors of the entrance. She looked around for them as the doors slid open. "Come on, girls, I thought you were in such a hurry."

They ran and followed her inside.

The waiting area had white walls and was filled with dark leather couches and plastic chairs. People were sitting in every possible spot. Some looked hurt or sick, while others were obviously relatives or helpers. Mrs. Buford led the way across the room to a long white counter with glass windows. A woman in a nurse's uniform sat behind one window.

"May I help you?"

"We're here to find out about Jennifer Smallwood," said Cindy.

"When was she brought in?"

"Just a little while ago."

The woman studied a list on the counter. "Yes, she's here. Are you family members?"

"We're just friends."

"What are your names?"

"Cindy Buford."

"Amanda Carter."

"Have a seat, and I'll send word back that you're here."

They turned back toward the waiting area. There were some brown-painted double doors beside the registration counter; another nurse appeared there and called a patient's name. Three people got up, and two of them helped the third limp painfully toward the double doors. Cindy, Amanda, and Mrs. Buford took their vacant seats.

On the wall above the registration window was a clock with hands pointed to eight o'clock. "I wish we could have gotten here earlier," said Jennifer.

"We had to cook and eat supper and clean the kitchen," Mrs. Buford reminded her.

It was a long wait. A nurse kept coming to the double doors and calling patients' names, and people from the waiting room kept coming and going through the same door. Mrs. Buford found change for all of them to have sodas from the machine in one corner. Cindy and Amanda had a little money in their pockets and bought one bag of potato chips to share. Two different times, ambulances arrived outside and medical attendants brought people on stretchers through the sliding doors, but took them down a hallway instead of into the waiting room.

Finally Mrs. Buford said, "We have to go. It's almost nine o'clock. I have to get up and go to work tomorrow."

"Can't we wait just a little longer?" Cindy begged.

Her mother scowled. "Five minutes. That's it."

It was a long five minutes. Cindy and Amanda stared at the second hand on the wall clock the whole time. Apparently Mrs. Buford did too, because when the five minutes were up, she stood.

"Time's up. Let's get moving."

Reluctantly the two girls left their seats and began to follow her toward the sliding doors. Cindy kept watching those other, brown doors. As they were about to leave by the sliding doors, the brown doors opened and a tall couple, both with blonde hair, came through.

"It's Mr. and Mrs. Smallwood!" exclaimed Amanda.

They glanced her way. Mr. Smallwood smiled tiredly and led his wife around several couches to reach them. She looked elegant in a pale blue cotton dress and white high-heeled sandals, but her upswept hairdo was a little messy.

"Nice to see you both," Mr. Smallwood greeted them.

"Amanda and Cindy, isn't it?" Mrs. Smallwood took Cindy's right hand and Amanda's left into her own. "Thank you so much for coming to see about my daughter."

Cindy said, "Thanks, we wanted to come. This is my mom, Mrs. Buford."

Mr. Smallwood shook her hand. "So nice to meet you, Mrs. Buford. I'm Roger."

"Please, call me Valerie."

"And I'm Lorraine." Mrs. Smallwood shook her hand too.

The two girls spoke almost together.

"How's Jennifer?" asked Cindy.

"Have you heard anything?" asked Amanda.

"She's up in X-ray right now."

"Is she still unconscious?" asked Amanda.

"She woke up but was in a lot of pain. The doctors gave her some medication."

"What do they think is wrong with her?"

Mr. Smallwood paused and looked at each of them. "They think her back might be broken."

The three just stared at him. Then Cindy clapped her hands over her eyes. "It's my fault!" she shrieked. "It's my fault!"

People in the room stared at her. Mrs. Buford put her hand on Cindy's shoulder. "Cindy, it is not."

"Yes it is!" she sobbed. "I told her to meet us there. She wouldn't have come otherwise."

"To the contrary," said Mr. Smallwood, "Jennifer was quite determined to meet you at that corner this afternoon. The police who interviewed you and all the other witnesses told us Jennifer wasn't careful and she skated into the street without looking."

"She did look!" insisted Amanda. "The car just zipped up out of nowhere. It was the same car that killed Mary Jo Green!"

"Who?"

There was a pause. Mrs. Buford sighed. "This dead woman they're obsessed with. She used to skate at the roller rink and she was killed last year at that same corner."

"By the same dark blue car," said Amanda.

Cindy's sobs subsided as she watched her mother from the corner of her eye. How much did she know?

Mr. Smallwood looked thoughtful. "Was that the car that Jennifer had me trace?"

"That's the one."

"And you think that car came back and hit Jennifer."

"No, the car didn't hit Jennifer."

All the grownups looked mystified. "Then what did?"

Cindy and Amanda looked at each other and kept their mouths clamped shut.

Mr. Smallwood grew agitated. "Look, witnesses told the police the car hit Jennifer, and they said the man who was driving used to live in that neighborhood. If somebody else did it, I want to know about it!"

Cindy forgot about crying. She and Amanda stared wide-eyed at Mr. Smallwood's angry face.

Finally Amanda said, in a barely audible voice, "Mary Jo Green knocked her down."

"Who?"

"The dead lady. She knocked Jennifer down. To protect her from getting hit by the car."

Now the grownups stared at her in astonishment.

"This dead woman is not really dead, but still alive?"

"No, she's dead," said Cindy. "It was her ghost. She wanted us to find the car that hit her. We did, and it came back again. She knocked Jennifer out of the way so she wouldn't get hit and killed by the same car."

Mrs. Buford rolled her eyes toward the ceiling, and Mrs. Smallwood looked confused. Mr. Smallwood sighed. "Well, everybody else says it was the car that did it."

"Nope," said Cindy decisively.

Mr. Smallwood's mouth quirked slightly. He said, "We have to go see about our daughter. It was nice to meet you, Valerie."

"Nice to meet you too, Roger."

"I'll be along in a few minutes, Roger," said Mrs. Smallwood. He crossed the big room and disappeared through the double doorway.

There was silence while no one could think of anything to say. Then Mrs. Smallwood said, "I hope you girls will come see Jennifer after she gets home from the hospital."

"Of course, we'd love to."

"Can we call in the morning to find out how she is?"

"Certainly. Roger and I are staying the night, at least until we hear some results, but we'll keep our housekeeper, Mrs. Smith, informed. We'll make sure she knows to tell you how Jennifer is doing."

"I guess we'd better go, then," said Mrs. Buford. "It was nice to meet you, Lorraine."

"You too, Valerie."

"Goodbye," said Cindy and Amanda together.

Cindy looked back as they walked away. Mrs. Smallwood was watching them go, but Cindy didn't think she even knew what she was looking at.

As they crossed the parking lot, Mrs. Buford spoke in exasperation. "One of these days your imagination is going to get you into real trouble, Cindy. Who do you think is going to believe a story like the one you were telling? And why don't you want that man caught?"

Cindy argued, "We do want him caught! But he didn't hit Jennifer, just Mary Jo Green and that fire hydrant on the other corner!"

Her mother shook her head. "Somebody could get hurt because of you."

Cindy began crying again. "Somebody already did. What if Jennifer's back is really broken?"

●●●

Cindy thought she would not be able to sleep, but the excitement of the day had worn her out, and she fell asleep soon after she went to bed. The next morning she woke up at eight-thirty -- early for her. She called Amanda.

"Have you talked to the Smallwoods' housekeeper?"

"Not yet. I was waiting for you."

"Let's hang up and I'll call." Cindy dialed the Smallwood's house number. The elderly lady's voice answered.

"Hi, this is Cindy Buford. I was wondering—can you tell me how Jennifer is doing?"

"Mr. Smallwood called me this morning. He said the doctors have read the X-rays and nothing's broken. Her back's just badly sprained and bruised."

Cindy felt relief seep through her entire body. She laughed out loud. "How soon can she come home from the hospital?" she asked excitedly..

"She has to stay long enough to make sure there are no internal injuries, but the prognosis is good."

"The what?"

"It looks as if she'll be all right."

"Can we go see her?"

"She can't have any visitors until tomorrow."

"Thank you, Mrs. Smith. Goodbye."

"Goodbye."

• • •

Jennifer's white silky nightgown was decorated with lavender flowers and her hair was in a ponytail fastened with a lavender clasp. Her outfit was pretty, but best of all were the rosy cheeks and the open eyes that sparkled a deep, dark blue. Jennifer's appearance was a great contrast to the blanched, bloodless face they had seen two evenings before when she had been loaded into the ambulance.

Cindy and Amanda shared one hospital chair while Cindy's mother occupied the other one.

"This is a very nice room," commented Mrs. Buford.

Cream-colored wallpaper and matching curtains made the place seem homey. A television set was on the wall across from Jennifer's bed.

Her mother, she said, had gone down to the coffee shop.

"My mother insisted on a private room. She didn't want anyone else to bother me." Jennifer sighed. "But the doctors and nurses are always asking me questions and doing tests."

"I'd go nuts," agreed Cindy.

"We do have more information on that car that almost hit you," said Mrs. Buford.

Cindy and Amanda began speaking at the same time.

"He was nuts! People said he was waiting in the library parking lot. I bet he thought Mary Jo would be out walking Mitzi again even though she's dead!"

"The blue car was his but he gave it to his brother-in-law to use and he borrowed it both times!"

"Girls, please." The two stopped talking and Mrs. Buford went on. "They haven't caught Jonathan Leifer yet, but it's only a matter of time. He abandoned his blue car down where Turnberry joins the main highway back to Baltimore. The police are searching for his red car."

"My father told me all that yesterday. What in the world was he planning?"

"No one will really know until he can be questioned. But according to his brother-in-law, a year ago Jonathan Leifer said he had a girlfriend who was cheating on him, and he needed to use the blue car to follow her without her knowing it. This year he gave some other reason for borrowing it."

"Mary Jo was never his girlfriend!" stated Cindy.

"We don't know that," said Amanda. "Rose said he pestered Mary Jo and she rejected him, but maybe she didn't reject him after all."

"Well," continued Cindy's mother, "right now he's just the owner of a suspicious car that struck a fire hydrant and left the scene of an accident. Cindy was right: no car hit you, Jennifer, and as far as anyone can tell, you just fell."

Jennifer nodded. "That's true, the car never actually hit me."

"It would have hit you if it hadn't been for—"

"Shh!" said Amanda.

After a moment Cindy asked, "So why did he run off? And why did he abandon the car?"

Amanda snorted. "So he wouldn't get caught, of course!"

"Hello," said a woman's voice. Mrs. Smallwood came into the room. Her blond hair was up in an elaborate hairdo, and she wore a soft, thin, long-sleeved mauve blouse with a low-cut neck over mauve plaid slacks. Cindy noticed that the colors went well with the curtains and wallpaper.

"Hello, Lorraine," said Mrs. Buford.

Said Cindy, "We were just telling Jennifer some things the police have learned about that car that almost hit her."

Mrs. Smallwood shook her head. "Oh, please, no. I've been so distraught the past couple of days, I can't bear to think about it." She looked very pale under her makeup, and there were dark lines under her eyes.

"Well, we won't talk about it any more," Mrs. Buford said cheerfully.

"The girls probably would like to visit for a while. Would you like to come have a cup of coffee?" Mrs. Smallwood almost seemed to be begging, as if she really needed company.

"Didn't you just have some?"

"Well, yes, but . . ." Her voice trailed off.

Cindy's mother stood up. "Girls, we're going for a walk. I'll be back in a little while."

The two mothers left the room. Cindy waited until their voices had faded away. Then she asked, "Do you think they'll ever find out what really happened?"

"You already told them and they didn't believe you," answered Jennifer.

"How do you know that?"

"I heard my parents talking when they thought I was asleep."

"How long do you have to stay here?" asked Amanda.

"They have some more tests to run. They took x-rays and can't find any broken bones, but my back is bruised and it hurts to move around."

"Will you have to stay in bed when you get home?"

"Yes, and I can't do any skating or exercise for at least a month."

"You'll go nuts."

"Probably."

"We can come over and visit you every day! If your mom will let us," amended Amanda.

"Would you? That would be so great. I hardly ever have company."

"Too bad Mary Jo never made it to a hospital."

They grew quiet, thinking. Then they all began talking at once.

"Did you see what Mary Jo looked like? Like she was on fire or something?"

"Did she really push you back across the street?"

"Did Rose see her? Did any of the other people who were around?"

"I thought no one else looked at her or tried to talk to her."

"Do you think Jonathan Leifer saw her?"

"I'll bet he did. I'll bet she wanted him to."

"Do you think she was trying to make him have a wreck and get killed?"

Cindy shook her head. "I don't think she was ever that mean."

"No, huh-uh. She wouldn't have done that." Amanda spoke with certainty.

"Well, I don't know if she was mean or not, but I was scared of her in the woods."

"She wasn't trying to frighten you."

"I hope not. Anyway, now she's happy, and she's probably gone for good."

"Are you sure she's happy? I think a better word would be satisfied."

"Satisfied." They thought about that word. "Maybe she is," agreed Cindy. "But I'm going to miss her if it means she won't be back."

Mrs. Smallwood and Mrs. Buford reentered the room. "Who won't be back?" asked Valerie Buford.

The girls looked at the adults. Nobody answered a word.

Chapter 18
Back in School

Victor stopped the white Cadillac before the columned porch. The three girls piled out and ran up the front steps of Smallwood Mansion, while Victor drove the car around the circle and back toward the garage in the grove of maples.

Cindy, Amanda, and Jennifer dropped their bookbags onto the floor inside the front door and started down the hall past the huge staircase. Cindy almost began running, but Amanda poked her in the arm and she remembered to walk sedately like Jennifer.

Mrs. Smallwood greeted them from her seat at the kitchen table. "Good afternoon, girls. How are you feeling, Jennifer?"

"Hello, Mrs. Smallwood," answered Cindy and Amanda. Jennifer walked over to her mother and hugged her; in return she got a kiss on the cheek.

"Just fine, Mom. Hello, Mrs. Smith," Jennifer said.

"Hello, Jennifer," said the white-haired housekeeper. "Hello, girls."

"Is there anything to eat?" asked Jennifer. "It's been three hours since lunch."

"I wish you got a healthy snack in the afternoon as you did at Fitzhugh Academy," Mrs. Smallwood commented disapprovingly. She continued, "We have fresh fruit salad and graham crackers with milk to drink. Would anybody care for some?"

"I would!" Amanda and Cindy shouted together.

"Yes, please," answered Jennifer.

The girls took the three empty seats around the table. Mrs. Smith brought four small bowls filled with freshly sliced strawberries, grapes, and different kinds of melon balls. Then she supplied spoons, a plate of graham crackers, and three cups of whole milk.

Cindy wanted to dig right in, but remembered to wait until everything had been served, and then to wait until Mrs. Smallwood began eating.

After a few bites, Mrs. Smallwood asked, "How was school today?"

"Great!" answered Amanda.

"We're going to dissect frogs in biology class soon."

Mrs. Smallwood closed her eyes. "Please, dear. Don't speak of such things while I'm eating."

"Sorry." Cindy hung her head and slurped another spoonful of sweet fruit.

"I'm enjoying it," answered Jennifer. "Going to Murrayville Middle School, I mean. The people are friendlier there."

"Don't you have to worry about misbehaving boys? I've heard they become very obnoxious about age 13. You never had to put up with that at your all-girls school."

"Well, so far we haven't had any problems," Jennifer answered.

"And if any *do* bother us, I'll make 'em real sorry," put in Cindy. "Ow! Don't kick me!" She glared at Amanda.

Mrs. Smallwood began to laugh. "I've heard how good you are at protecting yourself, Cindy."

Jennifer looked at the kitchen wall clock. "It's almost four. We need to go upstairs."

"You know what to do with your dishes."

They rinsed their empty cups and bowls in the sink, then stacked them on the draining board. "Thank you, Mrs. Smith," said Jennifer, as she was leaving the room. "Thank you," chorused Cindy and Amanda.

"You're quite welcome, girls." Mrs. Smith was already beginning to wash the dishes with a soapy sponge under water running from the tap.

They took their bookbags up to Jennifer's room, then sat on the carpet and waited for Jennifer to turn on her newer, bigger television. Her parents had bought it the previous month, when she'd had to spend so much time in bed after her back injury.

The sound came up first, then the picture. And there was T-Bird sitting on a couch, being interviewed by an afternoon talk-show host.

T-Bird's hair was longer now, and cornrowed in a style very similar to Amanda's. She wore an all-pink outfit: pink tube top with matching shorts, even pink tennis shoes.

"Ooh, she's dressed to look like me!" Amanda exclaimed. Then she frowned. "She looks like a brown-haired Barbie doll. Do I look like that?"

"No, you don't. She's more like a baby doll," commented Cindy. "Is she trying to be a tiny kid again?

"It's just a look," answered Jennifer. "People in show business try different looks all the time, just like ice skaters do."

"Roller skaters, too," put in Cindy.

T-Bird was talking about her new album. "My music is going in a whole new direction. I'm trying for greater maturity in my creativity. It's time to put away childish things and grow up."

"Hmm," Cindy said quizzically. "It's time to dress that way, too."

T-Bird and the host chatted a little more. Then T-Bird jumped up and ran across the stage to stand in front of her all-girl band and backup singers.

"Now we get to see and hear her new video," Cindy said excitedly.

The drummer set the beat. Then the guitarist and keyboard player joined in. T-Bird was dancing lightly the whole time.

"I don't guess she's going to put her skates on for this one," said Cindy.

"Well, she can't skate in every video," answered Amanda.

"She only skates in one of them. But that floor looks too slick."

The song was called "Only U." T-Bird hadn't been singing long when the live action began cutting in with shots from the video.

"Oh, my gosh!" exclaimed Jennifer. "She's ice skating!"

It was true: in the video shots, T-Bird was in an ice rink and spectators were watching from the stands, clapping and cheering. Her band and singers were at one end of the surface; they were not dressed warmly and Cindy wondered how they could stand the intense cold. T-Bird's appearance kept changing: sometimes she was wearing a hockey uniform and avoiding other players as she tried to whack a puck into a goal with a hockey stick. Other times she was wearing black leggings and sweater and skating with a young man who looked as if he knew what he was doing. It was sort of like free dance, but T-Bird couldn't do the same moves on ice that she did on rollers.

Jennifer shouted again. "That's Ron Haven! He used to skate pairs and now he's with Scott Hamilton's ice show!"

"Wow, look at that. He lifted her and it looks pretty good."

Mrs. Smallwood appeared at the door into Jennifer's bedroom. "What's going on?"

"Mom, look! Ron Haven is ice skating with T-Bird!"

"T-Bird? That singer you like? I thought she was a roller skater."

"She does everything," Cindy announced proudly.

Mrs. Smallwood sat on the bed and watched the rest of the performance, which ended with T-Bird and her band bowing goodbye from the studio stage. Mrs. Smallwood smiled. "Well, that was entertaining, though I can't say much for the singing. I could barely hear her voice, and I couldn't make out the words."

"I bet more people will start coming to ice rinks now that the ice skating video is out," defended Cindy.

"And that might not be such a great thing," Mrs. Smallwood said wryly. "Sessions are already too crowded." She started for the door. "I think you girls need to get busy on your homework now."

"Yes, ma'am." Jennifer shut off the television and they pulled biology workbooks from their respective bags. Jennifer sat at her desk while the other two lay on the floor to study.

"Did you get number ten?"

"It's easy. The teacher told us the answer in lecture."

After about forty-five minutes, Cindy and Amanda packed their books into their backpacks. It was a few minutes past five o'clock.

"So, let's see—tomorrow's Friday," said Amanda, shouldering the heavy bag. "Do you go to your father's for the weekend?"

"No, that's next week," answered Cindy.

"So you can come to *my* house tomorrow after school."

"I have ice skating practice," said Jennifer, "so I can't come."

"What about the roller skating session Saturday afternoon?"

Jennifer was walking Cindy and Amanda down the stairs. "Maybe. I don't know if I can practice two days in a row yet." She added thoughtfully, "I'm actually thinking of taking roller skating lessons."

Cindy was startled. "Really? You'll switch?'

"Well—maybe not switch. Or not completely. Maybe do both."

"Would you compete in both ice and roller?" asked Amanda.

"I just want to learn how to do freestyle on roller skates. I might never enter a competition."

They reached the front door. Cindy and Amanda said goodbye. Jennifer watched as they descended to the circle, rounded it, and started down the long driveway toward Smallwood Lane. Then she closed the door and went back to finish her homework.

Out on the drive, Amanda commented, "If your mom hadn't gotten that promotion, you'd be living in Baltimore and only able to come here every other weekend."

"Don't I know it."

"Do you think Jennifer will stay in Murrayville Middle?"

"School just started a couple of weeks ago so I think it's too early to tell. But I think she likes it."

"But will her mother let her?"

"Only if she gets good grades and wins all her skating competitions."

"What about us?"

"We haven't entered any skating competitions yet."

"Come on! I mean will she let us come to Jennifer's house, and let her keep coming to ours."

"I think her dad wants her to, so I guess her mom will."

They chatted about school awhile. Suddenly they had reached the intersection of Turnberry and Smallwood Lane.

They stared into the street and across at the corner that was the last place Mary Jo Green had stood before she died over a year earlier.

Amanda glanced somberly at her watch. "It's almost five-thirty. "

"I know. But the sun is lower."

"It's September. The days are shorter."

"Do you think she'll come back?"

"We've waited around for her three times and she hasn't come back yet so I don't think she will today."

"Probably not."

A horn honked. They looked around, startled. A car was stopped in the opposite lane and the driver was motioning for them to cross. Several cars waited in a line behind it. The girls checked toward the bend where the road disappeared. In the low, bright sunlight, they couldn't see anything coming from that direction.

It seemed safe. Together they started across.

They passed through the lane nearest them, still empty on the left, then crossed in front of the waiting cars, and stepped up onto the curb at the entrance to Evergreen Woods. They waved to the driver who had waited for them, a man in a business suit, probably on his way home from work.

That lead car started up, then one by one the vehicles behind it, and soon all the vehicles had disappeared around the bend. Now traffic was coming from that direction as well.

"We could wait and talk to Rose Witcrest. She'll be along."

"Maybe. But Amanda, you know we both have to get home."

"Right. Be nice if Tayvon could be gone."

"Does he like preschool?"

"He likes driving the teachers crazy."

They followed the sidewalk toward Cedar Terrace. Now Cindy had questions. "I wonder if Mary Jo'll be back next year. Do you think she'll come here again?"

"I kind of hope so."

"She tried to do nice things for us even though she was dead and so I hope she's happy. That's what I really want."

"Yeah, me too."

They turned left at the entrance to their development.

Amanda said, "It seems like it only happened yesterday or maybe the day before and at the same time like it lasted all summer long. But it was only ten days from when you first met her until she left, and only five days from the time she spoke to me."

"Yeah, it's freaky if I stop to think about it."

They began to hurry. Amanda's mother would have supper ready, and Cindy's mother would be getting home from work soon. They reached the spot opposite Cindy's townhouse.

"See you in the morning."

"Yeah, see you."

Amanda ran ahead. Cindy looked both ways before crossing Cedar Terrace. When she reached her house, she paused to look back at Amanda running up her own front steps and inside her house.

Cindy surveyed her neighborhood. Kids played at the playground past Amanda's house. Cars passed along Turnberry. People arrived home from their jobs.

Cindy glanced at her chipped concrete steps and slightly rusty iron railings. Thoughtfully she grabbed one railing and pulled herself up to the door.

She removed the door key from her pocket and studied the shiny brass key as it lay in the palm of her hand. Then she slipped the key into the tarnished keyhole of the faded, peeling, brown front door. The lock turned easily.

Cindy slid out the key. She looked back one more time. Then she opened the door and entered her new, permanent home.

ACKNOWLEDGEMENTS

Thanks to:

- Jeanne Cavelos, originator of the Odyssey Writer's Workshop in Manchester, New Hampshire, for teaching me how to write down my nutty ideas
- The members of the Odfellows on-line critique group, alumni of that workshop
- Todd Supple and the WGFH critique group of Montgomery County, Maryland, for helping me iron out the bugs in this story
- Kitty Hopkins of Sharon Press, both for editing and formatting the manuscript and for photographing and designing the cover
- Ashley Earp, LaTreseBarker, and Kaitlyn Westcott-Tau for modeling for the cover
- Phil Nanzetta of Signature Book Printing for his patience in helping me print the book
- Ira, my husband, for believing in me
- God for making all things possible

Cover models:

1. Cindy Buford, In-Line skater
Ashley Earp -- 2005 Freshman/Sophomore B Pairs National Champion

2. Jennifer Smallwood, Arabesque
Kaitlyn Westcott-Tau -- 2005 Sophomore A Pairs National Champion

3. Amanda Carter, Speed skater
LaTrese Barker -- 2005 Juvenile/Elementary B Free Style Regional Champion